Fifty

Seventy

BarbarianSpy

BarbarianSpy
FOR LITERARY HEAT

www.barbarianspy.com

This book is copyright © habu 2014
habu asserts his right to be known as the author of this work.
Published by BarbarianSpy in 2014
Cover design © S Bush 2014
Cover images: all manipulated; man with tennis racquet and man with water bottle Copyright: photography33, man with beard Copyright: Goodluz, man on grass Copyright: monkeybusiness
E-Book ISBN: 978-1-922187-88-8
Print ISBN: 978-1-922187-89-5
All rights reserved

BarbarianSpy
Jindalee St
Toronto, NSW, 2283
AUSTRALIA

Fifty

Seventy

by

habu

CONTENTS

Introduction

We all grow old—if we're lucky—and, if we're honest with ourselves, we wonder if we will be one of the lucky ones one who can still get it up at ninety and enjoy a sex life. All of us who have enjoyed an active sex life wonder, with some sense of concern, how good sex can be at fifty, and whether there can be sex at all at seventy. And these are as much questions in the gay world as the hetero world. Add to that the question of the durability and sexual aspects of May-December relationships or, perhaps even more problematic, October-December relationships, and the concerns can be complex. But the possibilities can be interesting as well.

Fifty Seventy is a six-story anthology affirming and exploring the sexual relationships between men when one sex partner is fifty and the other seventy. These six stories are varied in not only time, place, and situation, but also in who is on top and who is on the bottom and how long their relationship has been going on.

7

All, though, share the common thread of a fulfilled sexual relationship among mature men of certain ages. All of these stories are of men still getting pleasure from sex in their later years.

The first of the stories, "Climbing Machu Picchu," deals straight on with lost opportunities and the call to experience experiences rather than standing off to the side and living them vicariously. "Footprints in the Snow" is a high-heat romp of a highly sexed fifty-year-old escaping to an isolated mountain cabin to dream his fantasies—and experience them blossoming into reality. "Play On" uses the venue of a grand slam tennis tournament to illustrate how a relationship, based on sacrifice, can develop into a continuing physical need. "Screw Too Old" is an in-your-face declaration of never being too old to enjoy sex. The final two stories turn more to the darker nature of the issue. "Tempting Memory" spends an evening with an aging rocker facing the impending loss of his even older lover, and "Tuscan Memory" is a bittersweet second bite of the apple, reliving a heated, forbidden summer fling.

Climbing Machu Picchu

"Some beautiful young men out there, aren't there?"

Alex looked up, startled. The man standing by his table at the edge of the verandah of the Southbeach Café, overlooking a stretch of Key West beach at the southernmost point in the United States, was somewhat of a cipher. He was clearly old—quite old—but he was equally clearly well preserved. His deep tan, tending toward the leathery, accentuated the silvery gray of his full head of hair and of the patch of hair on his chest as well. He had been a strikingly handsome man once and was still handsome in an arresting way—for his age. He also had been very well muscled and there was evidence of that still. The immediate impression he gave to Alex was of some sort of mummy of a man who had died in his prime and, although decaying, was doing it at glacial speed. He was just wearing baggy shorts and flip-flops. He was smiling, showing a set of gleaming-white teeth—impressive whether or not they all were still his.

"Beg pardon?"

"I said that there were some beautiful men out there playing volleyball. Many of them really sexy, all types represented, making selection easy."

"Yes, yes, I suppose. I was absorbed in the game."

"A big volleyball fan, are you?"

"No, not really, but—"

"I didn't think so. A professional observer are you?"

"Ah . . ."

"Do you mind if I sit, to take a load off. I've come to observe myself, for the moment, and this table has the best view of the beautiful young volleyballers."

"Yes, of course. Do join me." The man was being quite forward and candid, but this was Key West. Alex had read enough about Key West to know that little was hidden or kept in reserve here. And it didn't mean anything to him, of course, if the man wanted to come across as "out there" gay. It didn't have to affect how Alex projected himself.

The man sat down and ordered a whiskey, followed by a coffee, from a waiter, who clearly was familiar with—and indulgent toward—the old gentleman. The waiter was obviously gay too, in a limp wristed way that put Alex off a bit. Alex didn't want to seem that open about anything.

The old man pulled a packet of vibrant-colored cigarettes out of his pocket and was lighting up even as he asked, "Care if I smoke?" He didn't wait for an answer before going on. "My name is Bob. I trust that you're a tourist, coming for the first time to our little tropical paradise down here to . . . observe?"

"Yes, down from Delaware—Wilmington—to escape the winter. Stopped here on my way farther south. My name's Alex, by the way."

"Nice solid name, Alex. It suits you. You're a nice solid-looking man. Well put together. Staying at . . . ?"

"The Blue Marlin, just down the street on Simonton. Rather interesting. An old fifties-style motel, but they keep it up and emphasize the retro."

"Yes, I know it well. So, just retired from DuPont and decided suddenly to see the world? You look a bit young to have retired. More than a bit, actually."

Was the man leering at him suggestively? Alex chose to ignore any possibility that he was. Still, he felt a tightness inside himself—as if the old man was pulling at him to extract all of his deep, dark secrets. Then why, Alex wondered, was he proceeding to give up nuggets about himself? At the back of his mind, he kept wondering just why it was that he'd wanted to take a side trip to Key West on his way farther south.

"Not retired yet, but you hit it on the head with DuPont. Not DuPont itself, but one of the major banks in town. We do a lot of work with DuPont. I'm fifty—just turned. Looked around and decided I hadn't done much of what I wanted to do in life. So, I'm on an extended vacation."

"Ah, yes. Fifty is a dangerous age. I'm seventy myself."

"Seventy? I wouldn't have guessed." And, in fact, Alex wouldn't have guessed that. Sixty maybe. Certainly older than he was himself.

"I've done what I can to keep that from being a first guess. And you got bored up there in Wilmington did you? Made a list of places to see, and Key West was on the list?"

"Yes, Key West has always intrigued me."

"Yes, yes, it does, for a certain type of man."

Alex didn't quite know how to respond to that, but Bob saved him the trouble, continuing on with his probing. "Is Key West the only sightseeing destination on your vacation agenda?"

"This is just a stopover. I'm on my way down to Peru. Wanted to see Machu Picchu. It seems to be on everyone's bucket list."

"Ah. Rather unique, a stopover in Key West on the way down to Peru. When you get there, you're going to do what, take a flyover of the area? You're not going to climb to the ruins?"

"Yes, yes, a flyover, but how did you guess that?"

"I sense a pattern here. And, so, why did you stop over in Key West? To observe beautiful young men playing volleyball on the beach or to fuck or be fucked?"

"Excuse me?"

12

"We're an open and honest lot down here in Key West, Alex, and the key is famous for one thing, really. I just wondered where you were in life. It seems you've moved to observer from experiencing. I can understand that. I was in my fifties once, facing retirement, and suddenly realized I hadn't been much of anywhere. In my rather older age, though, I've discovered that it's all going to abruptly stop at some point—and I will either have collected photographs of others doing something—young men playing volleyball on the beach, for instance—or I'm going to have experienced life myself. That's why I went back to smoking and drinking . . . and fucking. And Key West is a great place to do all that and devil may care."

"Fucking at your age?" Alex asked, stung by what Bob had said and wanting to sting a bit back.

"You better believe it. And I'm quite good at it, if I say so myself. You're only fifty. You're not past it. And you're a good-looking man who has kept yourself in shape. There are a lot of fifty-year-old men fucking other men on Key West. It's what we're good at here. If you're brave enough to go past observing, you'll maybe admit to yourself that men don't come down to Key West by themselves just to observe beautiful young men playing volleyball on the beach."

Alex's ears reddened up. "Is this some sort of propositioning? If so, I must say it's creative."

"Yes, it is an invitation to fuck, Alex. You're a good-looking man alone on a beach in Key West, ogling young studs just in Speedos. Why wouldn't I be propositioning you? Life is too short to beat around the bush—although I'm not propositioning you for right this minute. I already have a fuck planned for this afternoon. I find you very attractive. You also don't fool me. Yes, I would like to fuck you. That's what I came down to Key West to do, why I live here now. I fuck younger men. And they enjoy me enough to ask for it again—sweet music to the ears of a seventy-year-old man."

"I don't really . . ." Alex tried to make his voice sound indignant, but he was more flustered and embarrassed than indignant. He had indeed come to Key West to recapture—in a voyeur way, he thought, when he thought about it—what he had enjoyed as a young man in his twenties. Not for the past two decades, though. He'd given all of that up to fit in and get ahead. He'd just come to watch, and no one had challenged him before on that being a mode of letting the experiences of life pass you by. He hadn't even looked into tours to climb to Machu Picchu. Why hadn't he even looked into that if he was going to make the effort to go there? And, no, of course Key West wasn't on a natural line from Wilmington to Peru. He had clearly fooled himself about that—and about how much he wanted to come to Key West and why. Why had he done that? Was he giving up? At fifty?

Bob had stood up from the table. "Not this afternoon. I can't fit you in this afternoon. But maybe we'll meet later, while you're still here in Key West, trying to live the lifestyle vicariously. Maybe we'll fuck then. I'm taking you for a bottom. Sorry, I only

14

top. For now, see that nice blond young man out there across the volleyball net, the one who looks more basketball than football? That's Trent. He's nineteen. He came to Key West to experience his dreams. The volleyball game is breaking up. I came here to watch him play. I'm taking him to my nice little bungalow on Amelia Street to fuck his lights out. That will be enough for me for the afternoon."

Alex sat there, stunned, as Bob moved toward the steps down to the sand. Bob's tone had been cheerful and casual. So why had Alex felt threatened by it? And he *had* come down here because of the men, and he *was* flattered at the compliments on how in-shape he'd kept himself so that, at fifty, he still could be desirable. So why was he upset at receiving a proposition, as strangely and baldly as it had been couched, from another man? The man was seventy; it should just be all talk. So, why did Alex find him—and what he'd said—arousing?

Bob stopped at the top of the steps down to the sand, turned, and said to Alex, "In case you wondered, I have eight inches, it still can get—and stay—hard, and I know what to do with it."

* * * *

"So, Alan, is it? You've come out to do some more observing? Is that all you're interested in yet, or would you like to

15

come back to one of the back rooms with me and Trent here for a three-way?"

Alex turned from where he was standing at the bar at the Bourbon Street Pub on Duval, to see that the strange old man who had propositioned him on South Beach that afternoon was standing there, his arm around the shoulder of that young blond man he'd said was Trent, and giving him a bright-toothed smile. Trent was smiling a bit dreamily too, and by the way Bob had his arm around him, it was obvious that Bob controlled him—and probably had satisfied him earlier in the afternoon. That was a bit of a surprise. Although the two had walked away from the beach restaurant together earlier that afternoon, Alex had half convinced himself that the old man had been putting him on—that he was the young man's grandfather.

"It's Alex," he said, finding that he wasn't being as cold and put-offish in his response as he intended to be. "I'm fine here at the bar," he added, not wanting to let himself reveal that Bob and his proposition—and his lecture about experiencing rather than just observing—had been all Alex had been able to think of throughout the afternoon as he hibernated in his room, arguing with himself whether he really was going to be brave enough to come check out the bars he'd been reading about—the gay bars. Alex didn't frequent gay bars, certainly not in up-tight Wilmington, Delaware. He didn't even know if there were any such bars in Wilmington—no, that was a lie, occasionally he checked out on line where they were and even sometimes drove by them. He could only fantasize about what went on inside them, though. Rooms in the back. Bob had mentioned rooms in the back. Alex felt himself, involuntarily, going hard.

"You go on back and find us a room, Trent, honey," Bob said to Trent, releasing the young man from his firm embrace. "I'll be along in a few—or maybe we'll be along. I want another drink—and to talk a bit with hot-looking Alex here."

Alex didn't think himself as hot looking. Certainly not at the moment. He'd come out in a sports shirt, linen trousers, and loafers, with socks. He could see now that that was decidedly overdressed for the gay stretch of Duval Street at night. Bob was still in his baggy shorts and flip-flops, but he'd pulled on an athletic T. In the dim light of the bar, he looked even younger and fitter than Alex had remembered him from earlier in the afternoon, in the unforgiving sunlight of South Beach. Trent, willowy, but firm-muscled and girlish-face handsome, was just in shorts—and barefoot.

Bob won't have much to strip off him to fuck him, Alex found himself thinking. And then he turned red and took on a sheepish look.

"Thinking of me fucking that sweet blond?" Bob asked, as the bartender delivered him a double-slug whiskey.

Alex blushed even more, as that was exactly what he was thinking. "No, I was thinking that maybe this wasn't really the place for me to be."

17

"The view isn't fine enough?" Bob asked, with a laugh. "They're practically fucking on the dance floor. And that little Latino on the dance pole looks mighty sexy. Don't tell me that you're backing away even from voyeur."

"It just isn't . . ."

"Isn't something you're brave enough to do? You're only fifty, Alex, and you're in good shape—fine-looking shape. You're not dead. And your momma ain't here—at least I don't see her here. Look at me. Look at my smile. You can still get it up, can't you? I'm seventy and I can. I'm about to go back to a room behind the bar and make that sweet blond cry. You decided to get off sittin' on the fence and just take the splash of getting off? You can go back there with me. I'll show you a good time. I can make you cry too, I'll bet. A good kind of cry."

"Uh. No thanks. It's kind of late, and this was my last stop. I think I'll go back to the—"

"Going on to Peru in the morning?"

"Yes, as a matter of fact—tomorrow afternoon. And I should be getting some sleep."

"Gonna fly over Machu Picchu or climb to it?"

Alex didn't know what he said to that. He disengaged as soon after that as he could, but, with a "Suit yourself, then" and a laugh, Bob was moving toward the beaded curtain-covered doorway at the back of the room before Alex turned in the other direction and escaped the bar.

18

* * * *

Alex went straight back to his room at the Blue Marlin Motel. Trying to wipe the thought of any encounter with the aggressive and forthright Bob out of his mind—not fully successfully, though, as images of Bob with Trent and then Bob with himself were floating through his mind—he busied himself in packing up for the flight back up to Miami and then on to Lima the next afternoon.

His hands were trembling as he packed, and he was muttering to himself, castigating himself. Damn that Bob, he thought, and then he adjusted that to damning himself. Why had he come down here? Was it just to observe and to dream as a voyeur? Hadn't hitting fifty given him a jolt about why he'd repressed himself the last two decades? He'd studiously kept in shape and he hadn't married or shown much interest in a relationship with a female all that time. What had he been holding back for, not fully giving up his dreams, his remembrances of how good it was when he was enjoying another man's body, another man's cock inside him?

The travel guides for Peru—for Machu Picchu—fell out of his carryon as he was pulling dirty briefs out of that to stuff somewhere in his suitcase and to replace with clean ones in case his luggage got lost in Peru and he had to live with the clothes he had in his carryon.

He took the guides over to the chair by a table in front of the window to the parking lot, the draperies now drawn, and sat down. He started looking through the ads in the guide again and the explanations of the tours offered. He couldn't stop his hands from trembling, though, and he threw the brochures down on the table in disgust and padded into the bathroom. He stripped and showered and pulled on a pair of sleeping shorts—all the time trying to keep images of Bob with Trent and Bob with him out of his mind. Unsuccessfully.

He heard a knock on the door when he came back into the room.

Of course it was Bob at the door.

"How did you find me?" he asked, both upset and pleased, and confused that he felt both sensations simultaneously.

"You told me where you were staying. I know the people managing the place. Don't you want to know why I came? Or do you think you already know?"

"I . . . I . . ." Alex was flustered. Did the man always have to be so blunt, so challenging, so suggestive—so knowing?

Bob held out his hand, revealing that he was holding a wallet. "Yours, I think. It was left at the bar. I recognized who it was from the driver's license inside. You really are fifty and you really are from Delaware. I'm impressed. I assumed you had made it up. Most do when they come down here to . . . observe. And I really did think you were younger than fifty. No matter there, of course. I'm really seventy, and fucking a man of fifty or a barely man of nineteen are both fucking a younger man. They both have holes to fill."

"I . . . I . . ."

"Are you going to invite me in? If you invite me in, I'm going to fuck you, you know."

Alex meekly stood aside, pulling the door wider open, and Bob strode into the room.

* * * *

The painful pleasure of it was excruciating. Alex had stuffed a folded sock from his nearby suitcase in his mouth to keep himself from raising the dead three rooms in any direction and, belly down on the bed and arms stretched up and out, fists gripping gobs of chenille bedspread, feet leveraging up and down off the carpet beside the bed, he endured the remembered ecstasy of a hard cock driving deep inside his ass. More than enduring it, he moved with it himself, leveraging off his feet, as he met cock thrust with pelvis thrust. This wasn't just Bob taking; this was the two of them fucking.

Bob wasn't just good, he was great. If Alex had remembered his life as a bottom in his twenties and early thirties as being this good and arousing, he never would have stopped. The rest of his life would have had to adjust to it.

Upon entering the room and after dropping the wallet on the table next to the travel guides, Bob had placed a hand in the center of Alex's chest and just pushed him back to the bed and into a sitting position. Alex had done nothing to resist, although he could hear the heavy breathing and the low-in-the-throat rattling sound, which he only vaguely connected to himself.

Bob had sunk on the floor between Alex's thighs, as, hands on Alex's knees, he pushed the thighs apart. Alex was already, suddenly, hard. His dick had pushed out of the slit of his sleeping pants. Not content with this, Bob pulled the shorts off Alex's legs and moved his mouth over the shaft. Alex moaned and his hands went to the back of Bob's head as the older man pushed the foreskin back with his lips, squeezed them tight on the rim of the bulb, and sucked hard on the bulb.

Alex convulsed wildly at the pressure on his cockhead, and Bob reached up with his hands and gripped the younger man's chest at the sides, under the armpits, and held him steady. Alex leaned back, his arms going behind him to support his weight on his whitened knuckles, threw his head back, and moaned deeply to the pock-marked ceiling. Bob's mouth went all the way down the shaft in a quick motion and then up slowly to return to sucking the bulb hard. Then down slowly and up fast, sucking the bulb hard. The pattern was repeated, again and again, as Alex groaned and shuddered.

The younger man hadn't had a blowjob in decades, and he'd never had one this good. He came quickly, down Bob's throat. Afterward he lay there on the bed, looking at Bob hovering over him, playing with a condom packet. Alex was effusively whispering his apologies for coming so quickly—and without warning and inside Bob's mouth. The older man said nothing. He just stood there, standing over Alex's body, unstrapping his belt, unzipping himself, pushing his shorts down, rolling the condom on his hard cock.

"Christ almighty," Alex whimpered with a shudder. "You weren't lying. God, I'm not sure I can . . ."

"I know you will. And you'll love taking every inch of it. Roll over on your belly."

With a groan, Alex did as commanded. The light next to the nightstand went off. They were in near darkness and would have been in total darkness if the curtains on the window at the front of the room met all the way.

For some silly reason, Alex felt more comfortable, somehow protected, in the darkness. It wasn't because he had been sucked off and was going to be fucked by a seventy-year-old man. Bob's body was fine. And that dick! Alex shuddered at the thought of it inside him. But, somehow, in the dark . . .

"Oh, shit, Oh fuck!" Bob was on his knees behind him, spreading his butt cheeks, rimming his asshole with his tongue, sticking it inside him.

And then the gigantic bulb of that monster cock was at his entrance, pressing in and out, testing him. And then it was entering him, relentlessly, as he writhed under the assault, thick and deep. Alex was gripping gobs of the chenille bedspread over his head with his fists and crying out. "Oh fuck, oh fuckkk! Go slow. Oh, shittt! Yes, Yesss. Fuck me!"

His eyes saw the folded sock, and he grabbed for it and stuffed it in his mouth, clamping down on it with his teeth, as Bob started to ride him hard and deep.

Later, Bob took him a second time, with Alex lying on his back, Bob holding his legs extended up and out, as Bob took him slower, exploring for and finding all of those niches and crannies inside Alex's channel that made him quiver and groan.

Then Alex lay there, moaning and sighing, as he watched Bob go to the bathroom. Alex didn't move—couldn't move as totally as he had been fucked by that big cock—while he listened to the shower. It wasn't long before Bob was back out of the bathroom, drying himself off. Still looking good for a seventy-year-old man, especially so in the dim light. His cock flaccid now, but hanging low.

"That was good," Bob said at last as he was pulling his shorts on. He hadn't been wearing briefs. "You're a good lay. You should be using your body, not holding it back. That's experiencing, not just observing. That's what you really came to Key West for, isn't it?"

Alex murmured something, he didn't know what. He still wasn't sure that's what he'd come to Key West for, but he couldn't disagree that that was what he wanted—what was missing in his life. He couldn't say he wasn't glad that he had gotten it.

Bob walked over to the table in front of the curtained window and picked up the travel guide. "Been looking at the tours again? Thinking of climbing Machu Picchu rather than just flying over it to see it?"

"Yes, maybe," Alex answered in a small, exhausted voice. His channel walls were throbbing. They wanted it again. To his embarrassment, if Bob told him he was going to fuck him again, now, Alex would have been exhilarated. He would have opened his legs and pull Bob's cock deep inside him. But Bob didn't do that. He was finished. He had made his point.

Bob sat down in the chair and picked up a small motel pad of paper and a pen and wrote something down. Then he pulled off the sheet of paper, folded it, and put it in Alex's wallet, which was still laying on the table.

"There," he said. "I know a guy in Lima. I think you'd enjoy him; I know he'd enjoy you. In case you want to continue experiencing and not only observing. In case you want to feel as young as I do when you are as old as I am. I think you can vouch now that I'm not past it."

Alex moaned. He certainly could. Again, his brain was screaming, Come over here and fuck me again. Put that huge cock up inside me and pump me to heaven.

"He's younger than you. But he has a big cock. I think we both know you want a big cock."

Bob stood then and put his hand on the doorknob. "Have a good time in Peru. You can find me anytime you want to come back to Key West. You're a good lay, Alex. Don't ever think you are past being wanted. Oh, and . . ." he continued as he opened the door and moved into the open space, "just to let you know, you didn't leave your wallet in the bar. I lifted it from you. I wanted to fuck you. Remember that. There are still men out there who will want to fuck you—for years more. We all die sometime. Don't do your dying before they start to shovel the dirt over you."

Alex's gaze went over to his wallet after Bob had gone. He already knew that he wouldn't be tossing out that slip of paper with the Lima contact address written on it.

Footprints in the Snow

"I have a cabin up at Massanutten. Why don't I give the key to that to you and you can go up there this weekend and just sack out?"

Reg3 was standing by my desk, having stopped in his periodic soaring through the offices, to notice that I was still in a morose mood. I was taken aback, though, both because he noticed and because he was suggesting that I could be two and a half hours away from Washington, D.C., at a snow-covered skiing resort, even on a weekend.

The word "soaring" had fallen into my mental depiction of Reginald Walker III's visitation to his Lobbyist firm's offices because it was descriptive. These offices were located in a Crystal City, Virginia, high rise overlooking a runway of the Ronald Reagan National Airport and, beyond that, looking to the dome of the capitol building and the Washington Monument obelisk across the Potomac. Despite his seventy years, Reg3 was still a soaring hawk, lean and mean and floating above it all, including his office staff, ready to swoop down and tear at someone's guts and dine noisily and lustily. No one in the office was fooled by the sweat-stained gym outfit he was wearing to "check in" on his office staff. He'd just been playing a vigorous game of squash, yes, but it had been with some senator or congressman or oil company lobby representative, and Reg3 had come away with more lucrative winnings for the firm than just a sports win.

By all appearances, Reginald Walker III was a one-man band of one legislation-influencing victory after another. Showing great stamina, he had been this energetic the entire twenty-six years I'd known and worked for him since I'd come out of graduate school at the age of twenty-four. But of course he didn't do it alone. His lobbyist victories were based on detailed research to provide a barrage of facts and secrets that Reg3 used to dive in for the kill just at the right time, at the right pressure point, and with the right argument.

I was one of those researchers. For twenty-six years I'd gotten little more credit than a nod and a vacant smile when I'd provided the information, enlightening or damning, it didn't matter which, that had enabled Reg3 to change some wavering senator's or congressman's vote on an oil bill. Yes, I'd been rewarded richly in monetary terms and in the perks of working in a high-powered firm in the nation's capital. But Reg3 was a hard and demanding boss—and he was all business. And he was ruthless in dealing with any employee whose impropriety led to his firm or himself being placed at a disadvantage in gloves-off, go-for-the-jugular lobbyist negotiations.

Reg3 was good at identifying who had really contributed what and to hand out generous bonuses appropriately and fairly, but he wasn't the one to know anything about the life of one of his employees outside of the office or to stop at someone's desk, note the family photos, and enquire after someone's wife or children. He expected an employee's life to be dedicated to him, Reginald Walker III.

Which made it all the more surprising that he noticed that I had been moping around the office for days—or, more surprising—that he cared enough to notice it and to offer me the keys to his mountain cabin and the permission to be more than a two-hour drive from his beck and call for a string of nights in a row. It was a Friday morning on the cusp of a three-day holiday weekend.

It actually sent a chill of apprehension up my spine. I had come to count on his disinterest in my life beyond the office. There was no framed photo of a smiling wife and children on my desk. If my boss had been more the observant and caring kind, I would have had to conjure up such a photo. There wasn't a photo because there was no wife and children. There only was a procession of younger men, men I picked up in gyms for their looks and their muscles and for their sexual preferences, men who were looking for someplace to live as they passed through the area from job to job—often, in my case, as personal trainers at the gyms I belonged to.

I was morose because the latest in a twenty-five-year string of these, Brad—the last in a progression of Brads and Chucks and Steves and Rods—had moved on, and not too amiably. I was fifty years old. I had reached a phase of looking for some form of stability, more a relationship than a progression of encounters that seemed like one-night stands even if the man fucking me was in my bed every night and had his own bureau and closet in my bedroom.

If Reg3 was more observant of a man who had worked for him for twenty-six years and had taken more interest in the few hours I spent away from his office and service, he certainly would have noticed that I was gay and opened my legs for a succession of bulked-up younger men. He couldn't have failed to link this with a chink in his office's armor to be discovered and used by the ruthless opposition at any moment—just as Reg3 didn't hesitate to use such information on the opposition himself, using data that underlings like me provided him.

"Are you sure, Mr. Walker?" I asked. "I would love to get away for a few nights, but with the wintery conditions out—and Massanutten could be completely snowed in—I would be out of touch."

"I'll be out of town myself for the long weekend, John," Reg3 said, not really focusing on me, his mind, as was often the case with him, skipping ahead to the next item on his agenda. But he obviously was serious, as he already was fiddling with a ring of keys attached to a loop in the waistband of his gym shorts. I held the prize in my hand while he wrote down the address of his mountain house and directions on a pad of paper on my desk.

He wasn't a bulky man, more lean and sinewy, but his hard-bodied musculature, clearly revealed in the T-shirt and gym shorts he was wearing—was apparent and proved out how active and energetic he was even at his age. My eyes couldn't help but follow the tight line of the meat of his thighs and calves as he leaned over my desk and wrote out the directions. There was a musky scent to him that brought to mind not only that he'd only recently come from a vigorous squash match but also that, at seventy, he was still a vital, virile male. It went with the territory of being a ruthless lobbyist in Washington, I thought.

Going to Massanutten really could put me out of touch with the rest of the world. The ski resort was a two-and-a-half hour four-wheel-drive trek in the snowy conditions of this Martin Luther King Holiday long weekend to the southwest of Washington, across the line of the Blue Ridge Mountains and nearly to Harrisonburg. I had been to the Massanutten resort before, but only in the summer months. It was one of the earliest minor ski resorts—mostly artificial snow and short runs—within a vacation-home strike for a busy and harried, but affluent, worker from the nation's capital. It had been designed and marketed heavily, but had been overtaken in sales decades ago by resorts offering better snow, longer trails, and more luxurious amenities.

So, despite being one of the first, from the early sixties, it was only about half subscribed and a time share could be picked up for the price of taking over the payments.

 Massanutten was a native American name that I had always thought of finding the meaning of—but never did. I did know it had been a sacred mountain for the Indians, the last peak running south on a spur off the Blue Ridge and pretty much running down the center of the Shenandoah Valley. I had always assumed it had been chosen for this spiritual purpose because of its shape. Although I was told it wasn't, I had initially thought it had been a volcano of ancient days, the Blue Ridge being the oldest mountain chain on the North American continent in geological terms. It looked like a small, long-dormant volcano to me, with its bowl exposed by a collapse of the rim on the eastern side. The result was a natural bowl at elevation with steep rims on three sides—which now supported short ski runs. The higher-rise time-share condos were located in the bowl and on the lower slope of the rim to the west along with the central club building, and the separate houses ran around on the slopes to either side and then down the mountain on spurs off the main road rising up to the bowl from the eastern side. Reg3's separate cabin was at the end of one of these spur roads half way up the northern rim.

 For me, Massanutten would be an ideal retreat. They didn't need artificial snow this week. There already were several inches on the ground in the valley below, most likely more already on Massanutten Mountain, and more snow was in the forecast.

This was Virginia, the upper south. It didn't take much snow and ice to make the roads hazardous, because there wasn't much reason to invest heavily in snow-removal infrastructure, especially in the rural and mountainous areas between Washington and the middle Shenandoah Valley.

I needed the isolation a snowy Massanutten Mountain promised—not to ski, but to hunker down in front of a fire and replan my future. Brad had been a life changer for me. For months I had thought—and planned on—Brad being permanent. He was at the upper edge of his bodybuilder phase. He still had great muscle tone, but he was balding and slowing down. He hadn't done anything more professionally than work in, and work out in, gyms. He had passed forty, and he'd need to find something to settle down to more permanently. I had offered him that, with me, and I thought he was good with it. But there was another man, a younger man, a richer man than me. And in just a few moments of screaming and packing, Brad had crushed my plans and dreams and was out of my life.

I was too old to go through this again. I needed to get away and rethink all of this. I was doing something wrong. I had no idea what it was. It wasn't my ability to support a man or my looks or my body or my talent as a bottom—at least yet, I knew. I had to rethink everything. The offer of a long weekend on a snow-bound mountain fell into my lap like manna from heaven.

"Thanks, Mr. Walker. I appreciate this."

33

"Don't mention it, John," Reg3 said, as he let loose of the edge of the paper he'd written the directions on and then gone over with me. And "don't mention it" fit the circumstance. His mind and attention already were someplace else—somewhere else for his brief hovering over the busy, heads-down staff in the office on a Friday morning in his periodic flight overhead to check out that all were busy and productive before he went on to his next squash match or hunting trip or bar cruising activity that only looked like he was at play when he was actually adding up the billables of his successful lobbying work.

I stood up and watched him float on down the corridor between the small office spaces, holding the precious key and directions in my hand. My name wasn't John. It was Sean. I'd worked for Reginald Walker III for twenty-six years, and still he couldn't remember my name.

I wasn't surprised. It went with the focused-on-cut-throat-business, dynamo that was Reginald Walker III.

* * * *

"Thank god for Chuck—or was it Steve?" I thought as I navigated my Subaru Forester along the ever-narrowing road—becoming more a track than a road—along the side of the ridge curving around on the northern side of the Massanutten bowl. It was getting dark, and I wanted to get to Reg3's cabin while I could still read the directions on the paper he'd handed me. I'd left the office right after Reg3 had. I was senior enough to come and go as I wished, and I rarely went before churning out ten hours of work. So I didn't feel at all guilty leaving early on the Friday of a three-day weekend. As it was, the rest of the office had started thinning out as soon as they heard the ping of the elevator taking Reg3 out of his realm. I went home and packed and was on the road south by 2:00 p.m.

I was thanking my earlier guys, whoever it had been who had given the advice, for telling me that, if I only had one car, even in the Washington, D.C., region, it should be four-wheel drive. The Forester wasn't flashy but it was reliable and I'd passed several nice sports car—and more than one SUV—in snow-bound ditches off to the side of Route 340 on my way down here. As it was, even the Forester was beginning to chug and catch occasionally on this spur road.

But then there it was, or rather they were. There were several undeveloped lots near the end of this spur road, but there, right where the directions said I would find it, was Reg3's log cabin, sitting well above the road on a pretty steep driveway. The driveway was asphalted, and it wasn't covered too badly with snow yet, that I could see, so I revved up the motor, turned left, and muscled the car up to inside a doorless carport underneath the log cabin, the first of two identical ones side by side on the road.

I had a slight scare right before I reached the base of the driveway. I was looking up at the house and rise of the driveway, estimating whether I should attempt the climb, when a blur of dark green slid out of the trees and onto the road to the left of me. Whatever it was, it almost hit the fender of the Forester before it turned and lurched back into the tree line. "A hunter, I wondered?" But I didn't think they would permit hunting inside the perimeter of the resort.

I called the house I was looking up at a log cabin because Reg3 had done so, but it wasn't the rustic structure I had expected. It was built of logs, yes, but it was one of those sleek Lindal cedar houses of thinner, more varnished logs and soaring roofs with large expanses of glass. My first thought was whether I was going to be able to keep warm in it.

That thought evaporated as soon as I entered the house. It was toasty warm, as if someone had come ahead and turned up the heater—a heater that worked efficiently. It wasn't hot, though, and my second thought of whether I'd have energy to set up a fire in the three-story rock fireplace I could see off to the right from the foyer was erased quickly as well. Logs were laid in the fireplace and, making sure the flue was open, lighting the fire was my first order of business before taking my coat and boots off.

The house was smaller on the inside than it appeared on the outside, this because most of the interior space, the living room to the right and the dining room to the left soared up two stories into a steep-roof ceiling in one open space. On the left, behind the dining room, was a large kitchen. Above the kitchen was a loft bedroom and bath, a balcony opened from the bedroom on one side to the living room and on another to the dining room. Two rock walls, more columns, separated the living room from the dining room. A staircase rose up to the loft directly from the foyer, climbing between the rock columns. Behind the living room was a commodious bedroom and bath. Completing the footprint to the left of this, behind the kitchen, was a screened porch. A rock wall faced both the far wall of the porch and the bedroom at the rear of the house, as the footprint for the house was cut right into the mountainside behind.

The house was tastefully decorated, but not overly decorated, in Southwestern style. There was beer in the refrigerator to complement the groceries I'd brought, and the built-in wine refrigerator was completely stocked. This was an expensively outfitted, but no-frills man's abode. I would feel the personality of Reg3 radiating from the house. In an off-hand manner, Reg3 had told me to be free with the liquor I found. I hadn't realized I'd find so much. There was a well-stocked bar between the dining room and the kitchen as well.

I found how to turn the music on and how to dim the lights. I didn't find any curtains to cover the soaring double-paned windows in the living room and the dining room, looking out, over the front deck, to the twinkling lights of the bowl of the mountain and the white stripes of the ski runs rising up the southern rim, across the bowl. I also figured out how to control the DVD part of the large-screen TV plastered to the rock chimney rising above the fireplace, and, just in a robe and with a glass of wine beside me and a flickering fire in the fireplace, I clicked into one of the several male porno DVDs I'd brought with me. I settled down to slowly masturbate my tensions away to a vid with a top who fondly and stirringly reminded me of the Rod of my experience of some twenty years earlier.

After my third glass of Shiraz and second ejaculation to the DVDs, I'd gone to sleep on the couch facing the fireplace. The fire was out and the DVD screen showing a pulsing blue when I woke. I closed up and went up to the loft, where I'd decided to sleep rather than in the first-floor master bedroom because the view out of the tall windows in the living room and dining room gave me a feeling of soaring out over the valley below.

I had intentionally not permitted myself to do any thinking about where I was and where I was going this first evening. I'd do my thinking over the next three days.

* * * *

Virtually the first thing I noticed when I woke up the next morning and stood, naked and stretching at the balcony overlooking the dining room, the downward-sloping and wooded front yard of the cabin, and the valley below were the footprints on the snow on the driveway, leading up from the road below and then back down again. It had snowed several inches in the night. The footprints weren't there when I had driven up the driveway—

I was sure of that. Of course, however, being sure didn't stop me from wondering how observant I'd been while muscling the Forester up the incline. They would have been right there in front of me, though. If they'd been there last evening. Not that it mattered if there had been footprints when I arrived. It had snowed in the night, a significant accumulation. No, they were fresh footprints—probably sometime this morning.

"Strange," I thought, "for someone to be walking up to houses out here near the end of a spur road." While mulling this, I saw the blur of a black SUV pass by on the road before me. This shouldn't have surprised me, but it seemed that I should recognize the vehicle from somewhere—but I didn't. It was bigger and boxier than most SUVs were these days, but it didn't look old.

I ruminated about both of these sightings while I sat at the kitchen table, drinking coffee, and chewing on a bagel. I came here to think deep thoughts about my life, but I found myself thinking about unexplained footsteps in the snow. And that blur of black of a car this far back on a spur road. There was that cabin next door, of course. That would explain that. Maybe even explain the footprints, although the houses were on the same level, with no obstructions between them. It wouldn't seem that someone going between the two houses would need to go down one driveway and up the other. Maybe someone was in residence in one of the other houses on the road and had some responsibilities for this house. The heat had been on and up to a comfortable level when I had arrived. Maybe there was a caretaker here of sorts. Reg3 hadn't mentioned one, though.

I found myself ruminating on what such a caretaker might be like. Would he be old or a young, fit man? I tried not to think that it might be a woman.

Then I thought back onto the previous evening. I'd slouched in a sofa, facing the fireplace, the lights dim, although there had been light, watching gay male porn DVDs, and jacking off—several times because I was highly sexed—in front of a nearly full-wall expanse of glass and no drapes.

I rose from the kitchen table and padded out to the living room. I was barefoot and only wearing sleeping pants. I told myself, as I carried my coffee cup with me, that I was only going to take in the view across the bowl of the mountain and down the valley, through the widely spaced tree trunks in the front yard, but when I got to the window, I looked down at the floor of the deck that ran across the width of the cabin. The footprints in the snow came across the deck and stopped in front of the window.

When had they been made? This morning, while I was asleep in the loft, or last night when I was masturbating on the sofa? How many times had I stroked off and shot off. Three? Four? I shivered and headed for the stairs to the loft. When I was fully dressed I came down the stairs and went back into the kitchen. I was putting the coffee cup and the plate from the bagel in the kitchen sink when I looked out of the window above the sink and into the screened porch at the back of the house. There were snowy footprints, not melted, because it was below freezing outside, on the floor of the porch—coming to this window and also to the door out onto the porch.

I went to the door and opened it, noticing that the lock seemed to be broken, that the door couldn't be locked. Sure enough, the snowy footprints had come to the backdoor, shuffled around and retreated. They'd also gone to the sliding glass doors—no curtains—to the master bedroom off to the right.

But I hadn't slept in that bedroom last night. I shuddered to think that someone might have been standing there, in the dark, watching me in that bed—if I'd been in that bed. I, of course, had masturbated again in another bed the previous night before going to sleep. I was highly sexed, even when I had to take satisfaction in my own hands.

I didn't know what I could do. I felt violated, but I had to laugh at that. I'd never felt violated by a stream of younger, hunky men doing far more than watching me nearly naked or masturbating before. It was mostly the strangeness and mystery of it that put me on edge, I guessed—and being out here all alone. And all I had to do was wear more clothes and keep my personal sex to the loft overhead. No one could see me in the bed up there. And there was a TV with a DVD player up there—and even a fireplace. I could spend the weekend up there.

I went back down to the dining room and looked down the length of the driveway that rose to the carport under where I stood, and contemplated the footprints in the snow again.

That's when I saw him—bundled up in a dark green hunting jacket and leaning on a snow shovel—at the base of the driveway. He started moving when he saw me standing at the window. I watched him trudge up the driveway, slowly, carefully, because the snow was several inches deep and who knew what ice there was lying in wait underneath? His footsteps followed, but didn't obliterate, the footsteps in the snow that had preceded his.

I went to the front door. I'd already ascertained that he was a hunk. A Hispanic maybe, or Mediterranean in origin. Built big and sold; thick, curly black hair pushing out from underneath the hood of his jacket.

His smile was tentative when I opened the door to him. "Open a door to him," I thought, already horny enough again to open my legs to a man. I tried to keep my own smile from spilling over the sides of my face. He was a young—maybe twenty-five or so—muscular hunk. I could tell that despite the bulk of his clothing. If he had been watching me last night . . . and if he knew and was knocking on my door . . .

But the footprints must have been made in the night. I didn't think it was snowing when I went up to bed.

"Hi," he said. "I saw a car in the garage, so I knew someone was here. I thought maybe you'd like to have your driveway cleared."

"Thanks, but I was thinking I'd go out and do that myself this morning. For the exercise."

Was I being too forward in drawing his attention to my conditioning. I was in great shape for a fifty-year-old. And I knew I was good looking enough, in a blond, Scandinavian way. A good contrast to his olive tones. My mind went off into flights of fancy of olive skin on milky white, hands gliding on curves and in crevices of contrasting color, my eyes latched on curly black pubic hair as my mouth sank down the sides of a brown shaft.

I shook my head to clear it. If I said I wanted to clear the driveway myself, would he just back off—forever. He was probably straight. You never could tell. But that was just it; you never could tell. "Of course I have no idea if there even is a snow shovel here. The house belongs to a friend. I'm just hiding out here—alone—for the long weekend. And I see that you came prepared . . . I mean that you have a snow shovel."

I checked his expression. Was that a slight smile when I'd said "alone?"

"How much would you charge?" I asked.

His face lit up then. So, he was offering because he could use the money. I wondered, briefly, what else he'd do for money. It struck me then that maybe that was a good part of my trouble with men—I threw money at them; I bought their hard cocks. Not time to think about that now, though.

He named a price, which was fine, and I left him to turn toward starting the job. He turned back then, though, and said. "I see there's no firewood stacked up here. The firewood pile is

43

against the side of the house. I could carry some of that up for you—enough to last the weekend."

"That would be good," I said.

"I could even bring some of it into the house if you didn't have enough inside."

"That would be nice too," I said. All of the signs were there. He'd even thought of a way to get into the house with me. "When you're done, I'll make you some coffee to warm you up before you have to go out again."

"That would be thoughtful," he said. A radiant smile before he turned back to the driveway.

Yes, I'm a quick thinker, I mused as I, reluctantly, closed the front door.

* * * *

The warming coffee afterward didn't work out quite as I expected. He did a quick job of the driveway and the wood and I saw that he was every bit the hunk I had estimated when he unburdened himself of a couple of layers of padding as he stood in the foyer and I admired what nature had formed.

But we didn't fuck.

I certainly wanted him to fuck me. He was a god in body and facial beauty, and he radiated a woodsy, fire-ash scent that turned me on—contrasting with, but similar in my response to the musky smell Reg3 had exuded the previous morning.

44

But we went no further than sitting at the dining room table, sharing a couple of cups of coffee and waltzing around the question of the bedroom. He was reticent and I didn't want to be the one to make the proposal. I laid a few hints, and he seemed to understand. But he didn't act on them.

"I'm Tony," he said. "No, I don't live in the area, not really, just moving through, and doing odd jobs here and there. Snow removal is there for the taking here on the mountain. Needed some cash to move on—toward D.C. or Baltimore or up the coast more, I guess. There should be work up there. I'm a carpenter; work in construction. Work with my hands."

I looked at his hands. Big, the fingers meaty and strong. I yearned to have them working my body.

The explanations came out in short phrases between sips as he did more looking out of the dining room window down toward the valley floor than at me, although I did my best to pose my body to the best advantage. When he looked at me, I maybe saw a bit of approval and interest, but I couldn't tell the nature of the interest. And I didn't want to be the one to make the proposal. Last night, to the extent that I had thought about where I was in life, I had come to the conclusion that part of the problem with me and my men was that I'd always been the one to make the proposal—to say I'd keep them financially, just in exchange for the sex. It hadn't been their fault to see it as a temporary arrangement. I'd set the conditions too low, and, from the beginning, I'd made clear that it was because I wanted it, needed it, had to have it.

If this Tony wanted it, he'd have to tell me. I didn't mind that it meant I'd be paying for it somehow. It already was an employer-employee arrangement. I had already given him money for the shoveling and wood carrying. And I'd added enough in a tip—enough for him to fuck me, as a matter of fact. But it had to be his move. The tip had been generous, whether I'd consciously piled it on or not. I did realize that this often was the approach—a generous tip to a personal trainer who I knew fucked men, for instance, was a recognized silent contract for added services. It always had worked before.

But he didn't make the move. He was polite and all and we got along just fine in discussion. But he didn't take me up to the loft and fuck me. More arousingly, he didn't bend me over the dining room table and fuck me right there. It was something that gave me pause in thinking he'd been a voyeur the previous night—responsible for the footprints in the snow up to the windows. And hadn't the footprints come after I'd gone to bed?

If he'd watched me last night, surely he could latch into the signaling today.

He seemed to be open with me until I'd quizzed him about where he was staying now. But he revealed enough for me to think he was camping outside, probably just inside the timber line at the end of the driveway. It was clear to me that he had been the one who had lurched out of the trees and almost into the

Forester the previous afternoon. And it explained the woodsy scent of a campfire on his body—and even that he had known where the firewood for this cabin had been stacked. He probably was poaching wood from the cabin.

I didn't probe, though. I didn't want to lose him, and I didn't feel a responsibility for Reg3's woodpile. I needed to find out if he would or wouldn't if he were cultivated more—if he had been the man of the footprints in the snow.

And I also had to acknowledge that maybe this was all just me falling apart up here, wanting a man's cock inside me, and having just lost my steady fuck.

* * * *

That evening I turned all of the lights on in the living room and stood naked, in front of the living room window, wine glass in one hand and dick in the other, and slowly masturbated—twice—for anyone out there to see, shooting my cum off in a splatter against the glass of the window, my eyes moving from the twinkling of the lights in the Massanutten bowl and valley below to the shadow of the trees, looking for movement. Not seeing any.

I went to bed, hyped up, not dissatisfied, though, because my mind was racing about the possibilities of what my exhibitionism might engender—especially in the mind and arousal of the Mediterranean hunk named Tony, who probably was camping in the cold snow at the base of the driveway below the

47

cabin. And who might be scouting around the house at night, looking for what he might see, what could give him pleasure. Leaving his footprints in the snow.

While I had been masturbating in front of the window, it had begun to snow, and it was accumulating nicely before I had shot off the second time. If it stopped snowing soon, I'd be able to check for footprints in the snow the next morning. I would know if anyone had been watching. Tony's feet were big and his boots had a distinctive sole pattern on them. I'd carefully checked that out when I'd had him in the house after he'd shoveled the driveway. I probably would know if the footprints were his.

I drifted off to sleep, masturbating myself before, completed once again, but not fully satiated, I rolled over onto my belly with a groan—not wearing the sleeping pants tonight. As I drifted into sleep, I conjured up the naked, muscular body of Tony—with me; beside me, stroking me with his hands as I reciprocated; under me, as, nose in curly black pubic hair, I sucked him big and throbbing; on top of me; inside me; fucking me hard, me bucking against him, crying out for the cock.

I moaned and raised my rump to him to give him a deeper angle. It was so beautiful, so real. And then I realized that it *was* real. I cried out as the cock withdrew, nearly the whole way, and then slammed down hard, deep inside me. Out and then in again. Strong hands were fisting my wrists, entrapping my arms above my head and spread, holding me gloriously in thrall to him. He was covering my back close, the hair on his chest scratching my back as his torso slid against me in rhythm with his cock pumping my channel.

I moaned a long, low, guttural moan, "Yes, yes, fuck me hard. Fuck me deep."

He growled into my ear, "More up on your knees, Sean. I can go deeper. You want me deeper."

Obediently, I raised myself more up on my knees and he was doggy fucking me. Hard, deep, pumping faster. I cried out in ecstasy.

"Yes, scream. Let me know you like it, that you want it. I've wanted to give this to you for so long."

I did scream out then, in passion and pleasure, bucking my butt back into him to meet his deep, hard thrusts.

I heard myself crying out, "Yes, god, Reg. Shit, yes. Fuck me hard."

I tensed with shock at what I'd called out. But of course I knew. I knew as soon as he began fucking me. The scent was musky, not woodsy; even in the dim light, I could tell the hands holding my wrists were not those of a young man; and the forearms were sinewy, tough, not smooth and hairy like Tony's had been as I watched him drink coffee at my dining room table.

I was being fucked by my boss, Reginald Walker III. And no matter how nonsensical that was, I didn't care. He could fuck every bit as well, could reach farther inside me even, could pump as long and as vigorously as any of the Rods, Stevens, Chucks, or

Brads I'd had inside me. In the dark, like this, he was giving me a glorious fuck.

Between fuckings—there were several that night; he was a virile man, and I was a needy bottom—he whispered, "Here, only here. But you will take the key to this cabin again, won't you?"

"Again and again, if that's what you want," I whispered back. At last, a man richer than me, a man who made the decisions and that I didn't have to proposition and be a sugar daddy to. Fuck being seventy. He had a big cock and still was able to do what he wanted with it—what I wanted from another man's cock. "But how . . . we're almost nowhere, in the snow."

"I own the cabin next door too," he said. "I came here as soon as I left the office—as soon as you accepted the key to this cabin. When I watched you stroking yourself to that gay porn last night, I was sure of you."

Of course, the familiar blur of a passing black vehicle. Reg3 owned a black Land Rover. I'd only seen it a couple of times, but it had registered in my mind.

"How did you? How did you know?" It hit me then that he'd called me Sean. He knew all along who I was. "You planned this. You set this up, didn't you?" We'd been side by side, but he was on his knees again, his strong hands on my hips, turning me onto my belly. I don't know if it had come out as an accusation. I didn't mean it that way. I was in awe of what he'd planned, that he wanted to fuck me. I realized suddenly that, over the years, I'd fantasized him fucking me, without ever having put the face and the name to the dream. The cock, though, and how it could make me both scream and moan, I knew all too well from my fantasies.

"This is just for here," he admonished me again, his status and reputation in Washington foremost in his mind. "You understand that, don't you?"

"I understand." It came out as a moan because of what his hands were doing as they explored my body. "But you set this up, didn't you?"

"Yes, I've been planning this for years," he growled. "But you always were with some younger man. Not now, though. You were mooning about being left. You were ready; you are ripe for it. You like my cock, don't you?"

"Oh, shit, yes, I love it. But I don't understand. You knew I was with men?"

"Of course. I know everything that goes on in the office, and don't you forget it. But this is completely separate from the office. Don't forget that either. Only here, but you'll be here when I want you, won't you?"

"Yes," I answered meekly—happily, even. A man to take care of me, to order me around. And one who could fuck like this too. That was what I was missing in my life. I knew that now.

"Up on your knees," he hissed, and exhilarated, aroused, I complied. I cried out in ecstasy as, gripping my hips with his hands and me fisting up wads of the sheets with mine, he thrust inside me again, immediately setting to pumping me hard and deep. I came almost immediately.

And later, I came again and again and again.

"I'll be back tomorrow night," he whispered as he pulled out of me for the last time and I could feel his weight lifting off the bed in the loft in the darkness.

"Please, please come earlier," I murmured back, in glorious exhaustion. "There's something I want."

"If you want," he whispered. He slapped me on the bare butt. "This ass is mine at last," he said with a low laugh.

"Yes," I agreed, with a sigh.

* * * *

Reg3 came after dark Sunday night, entering the cabin through the back porch and the kitchen door. It was snowing again. He surprised me by entering in the back and was already half naked before reaching the living room. Again I had all of the lights on and a fire going in the fireplace. I had hoped to see his boots, but he'd left them in the kitchen. I did see his feet, though.

He laughed when he entered the living room, to find me standing there, naked, my dick in my fist. "So, you want me to fuck you in front of the fire, is that it?"

"No, I want you to fuck me in front of the window," I answered.

He gave me a strange look and a crooked smile, but he did as I asked for the first fucking—we both knew we'd want as many fucks as we could manage, he to affirm his virility to himself each time as age caught hold of him, and me because I was so needy and, admittedly, because I was worried about the onset of age as well.

He fucked me from behind, him standing and crouched behind me and me with the heels of my hands and the knees of my widespread legs pressed against the window glass. As I was nearing completion, he reached around, fisted my cock, and finished me off, my cum again splattering against the glass of the window. He took longer to come, but he did so finally, starting with a grunt and releasing me so that I could sink to the floor and offer him a cheek while he ripped the condom off and ejaculated on my face.

"You want to do it in front of the fire next?" I asked.

"No. I want to use the downstairs bedroom. I like the mattress in there better than upstairs."

I had in my mind the whole time that I would check the new-fallen snow the next morning for footprints. It hadn't been just a whim that I wanted to be fucked in front of the living room window. But, although I did check, and found what I was looking for, I didn't really need to check.

Reg3 fucked me on the master bedroom bed, with me on my back, pillows under the small of my back to elevate my buttocks to a deep penetration angle, and Reg3 kneeling between my spread and raised legs and holding my ankles up and out with his encircling fists. He was spending enough time leaning down to nip at my nipples as he fucked not to see what I could see—my head dangling over the far side of the bed, staring through the sliding glass doors out onto the darkened screened porch.

Tony standing here, on the porch, near the door, just inside the shadows, fisting and stroking his cock as he watched Reg3 fuck me.

I opened my mouth in a broad "O," exhibiting my willingness, my desire, to give Tony suck. He moved, briefly, closer to the glass, which he splattered with his cum before withdrawing into the shadows and fleeing the porch.

I had seen that Reg3's feet were regular sized and I didn't have to check out the soles of his boots. I did find the footprints in the new-fallen snow the next morning, both on the deck in front and leading up to and inside the porch in back. The size of Tony's feet; sole prints to match the pattern of Tony's boots. But I'd already seen what I needed to see to be sure of Tony now.

Still, I was a bit surprised Monday afternoon as I drove the Forester down the driveway—hopeful but until then not completely sure—to find Tony waiting at the bottom of the driveway. He was all bundled up in his forest-green coat and beside him, on the ground, was a pack of camping gear.

He raised his hand as I reached the bottom of the driveway, and I stopped and rolled down my window.

"I want you to drive me up to D.C.," he said. I didn't hear much in the way of request in his voice. The commanding tone aroused and exhilarated me.

"Where in D.C.?" I asked, my voice full of hope.

54

"You said you have a house and that you roomed guys from your gym sometimes. We can go there."

"You want to room with me for a while?"

"I got your message this weekend. No playing games here. You take cock, I know you want mine, and I want to fuck you into next week," Tony said with a growl.

There it was. That's what I wanted to hear. It was nice to hear it from Reg3. But this was best of all. I hadn't lost my interest in young hunks fucking me. I just wanted one who pitched me, who would take control of me.

"Climb in," I said, but then I clarified that as he was moving around to the passenger door. "Climb into the backseat."

"The backseat?" he asked, raising an eyebrow.

"I'll take you to D.C.—and home—but I can't wait that long. I want you to fuck me right here, in the backseat of this car."

"Right out here?"

"I don't give a fuck who sees us doing it." I answered. "That is, if you don't," I continued, cautioning myself to let him control—knowing now that that was what I wanted from a man.

"Shit no, I don't care," he answered, opening my door, and, to my delight, manhandling me out of the front and into the back.

As I sat in his lap, our clothes only open enough to expose his thick, hard dick and my yielding channel, the car rocking up and down in the snow, he raised and lowered me on a divinely big cock and I ran my fingers through the thick, curly black hair of his head and turned my head up to the ceiling of the car to cry out my pleasure. I had already sucked his cock and found his pubic hair as thick and black and curly as I had imagined and his woodsy scent more intoxicating than ever before. While he fucked me, I had the presence of mind to thank either Chuck or Steve again. They hadn't just recommended I get a four-wheel-drive vehicle, they'd also said that the Forester had better springs than any of the others in its class.

Play On

The older man with the sinewy, grizzled body, baldheaded but with an abundance of salt and pepper body hair, and the younger man, barely more than a boy, tall and lanky and blond, met at the center of the net. The younger man, shirtless and in gym shorts and tennis shoes, looked wrung out and was hanging his head. He was covered in sweat and had a hangdog look about him. His hair was soaked and hanging down in his face. He obviously had been worked hard on the court.

In contrast, the old man, also shirtless and in gym shorts and tennis shoes, looked like he could go another couple of sets. He was lightly sweating too, but his body more glistened than melted under the burning Flushing Meadows sun. His body was hard, not massively muscled, but without an ounce of body fat on him. So hard that the bluish veins on his arms, legs and torso popped up just under the surface, there being no fat in his body for them to run through.

The older man was lecturing the younger man, demonstrating this and that with his tennis racket. The younger man was mimicking his moves and either nodding or shaking his head at the quiet instruction he was being given. After a bit, the older man reached across the net and cupped the back of the young blond's head and gave it a couple of pats.

They turned and walked toward the benches at the side of the tennis court, where their gym bags lay on the ground and various bits of tennis paraphernalia and backup tennis rackets were scattered along the benches. They were also walking toward a middle-aged man standing near the net post and just inside the wire gate to the corridor between this practice court and the one next to it. This third man, who was fifty, but a well-preserved, if slightly puffy, fifty, was wearing a light-green polo shirt over well-pressed khaki trousers. His brown-leather loafers looked like they'd cost a couple of hundred doors—each shoe—and, indeed they had. He was a handsome man with a full head of gray hair, but with darker eyebrows, a darker down on his forearms, and darker hair curling up from the V of his polo shirt, indicating that he once had been an auburn brunette. Twenty years the older man's junior, he hadn't sustained the hard body the older man had. He wasn't fat, but he was meatier and more pampered, treated more to massages than the blistering sun and the effect of pounding after tennis balls.

As the two tennis players reached the side post, the man who had been coaching the young player man reached over and slapped the younger man on the butt and muttered, "Get a shower, and then I'll see you in my office after I've had a chat with Mr. Sebastian here." His voice, a deep bass, was heavily accented. Either Russian or of some eastern European origin. In fact, it was Russian, retained despite fifty years residence in the States.

The young blond flashed Sebastian a look laced with curiosity, interest, and a hint of recognition. He then went over to the bench, scooped up his tennis gear, and sauntered off toward a long, low building set in the middle of a sea of practice courts.

The two older men watched him go, and then Sebastian turned to the older tennis player. "Wasn't that Gordy Patten, Grigor? Didn't he go out in the first round?"

"Yes it is Gordon Patten, and yes he did get beaten in the first round. You may remember him from the academy, although he was just a kid then. Took a set, though, which is better than last year."

"I heard you tell him to meet you in your office. They've given you your own office here?"

"Including your Stephanie, I have seven in the tournament, so I get my own office in the locker room here, yes."

The older tennis player and coach, Zhukov was standing close to Andrew Sebastian, and Andrew trembled at the sensation that the older man would reach out and touch him. The Russian tennis coach had always been the hands-on type. Andrew couldn't decide whether he would shrink from the touch or warm to it. The two men hadn't spoken in person for five years, and the parting had been somewhat volatile. And then the Russian did reach out and touch Andrew on the forearm, leaving his fingers there, as they continued to talk in somewhat strained tones. A chill went up Andrew's spine at the touch, and the sensation fought for his attention as they continued to talk in low tones, even though there wasn't another soul in sight.

"That was two weeks ago when Patten lost," Sebastian said. "First day of the Open. I'm surprised he's still here. So, he's still one of yours? I would have thought—"

"Yes, I have him at academy still—and it has been years, I think, since you have come to Boca. Even Stephanie notices that and remarks on it—somewhat bitterly, I might say. Not good; not smart. But on Patten. His backers won't release him from my academy 'til I say he's ready to go on his own. I told him second round at the U.S. Open this year or back to Boca Raton. So, is back to Boca Raton."

"But not last week?"

"No. He stay here and watch how others do it—others who can get past first round. And I work him every morning, here, until he ready to fall, until he look good enough to make it to second round in Melbourne in January."

"I'm glad you weren't that hard on the women players, Grigor." Sebastian said, with a somewhat nervous laugh.

60

"Stephanie never complains to you does she, Andy?"

"No, Stephanie never complained to me about you. She has always sung your praises."

"And now she in the women's finals, this afternoon."

"Yes, yes, she is. Against your own daughter. How do you feel having two of the women players you trained, including your own daughter, in the women's final of a major?"

"Is about time, don't you think?" Grigor Zhukov answered. "How do you think I feel? Proud, of course."

"But it means so much to you—what you want from me—to do this?"

Zhukov just gave Sebastian a hard look, and when he next spoke, he changed the subject altogether. "Must go now, Andy. I see you later. Instruction of Gordy not over yet."

Andrew Sebastian returned the hard look, started to say something, thought better of it, and then turned and walked to the open gate to the pathway between courts.

"I see you later, right?" Zhukov repeated, his voice a bit deeper and harder than the first time he'd said it.

Sebastian visibly sighed and answered, without turning back. "Yes, later." And then he left, walking in the opposite direction to that Gordy Patten was taking to the locker rooms. Going instead toward the main part of the tennis complex of Flushing Meadows, where his daughter and Grigor's would be battling it out later that afternoon for the women's tennis championship trophy at the U.S. Open.

Zhukov watched him go until he'd turned a corner at the edge of the practice court compound and was out of sight, and then he walked slowly toward the locker room. He wasn't in a hurry. He did his best not to wince as he walked. At seventy, he knew he was getting too old for this hands-on tennis instruction. But with him, it would be hands-on or nothing.

He entered the locker room and looked around, not seeing anyone. It was the last Saturday of the tournament. It was all over except for the two championship matches. The two men would be out here, practicing, this afternoon, wanting to do so when all attention was on the court where the two women were playing their final match. They'd both sleep in this morning, though, willing their bodies to recover from the two hard-fought weeks of getting this far.

He passed the shower room, the shower still dripping where Gordy Patten had just been, and entered his temporary office, at the end of a corridor, back in a corner, just like he'd requested. There was a window in the door. All of the doors had windows in them. But he'd covered his on the inside with paper and no one had questioned him. Once in the door, and having closed it behind him, Zhukov stood there, looking at the young tennis player, Gordy Patten, perched on the edge of a massage table, naked except for a towel wrapped around his middle.

Zhukov shot the bolt of the door lock behind him and moved to the table.

Neither of them spoke. This was nothing unusual. This had gone on since he turned eighteen while Gordy trained at Zhukov's Boca Raton tennis academy—just part of the payment for Zhukov developing Patten into a tennis star.

Reaching the younger man, Zhukov reached down, placed his hands under Patten's knees, and lifted the young man's legs off the floor, spreading them and raising them to where the heels of Patten's bare feet could dig into the edge of the padded table top. Patten himself unknotted his towel, opened it, and spread it out on the surface of the table top on either side of him. He leaned his torso back, his shoulders pressing into the cinderblock wall on the far side of the massage table, and moaned to the ceiling as Zhukov's tongue went below his ball sac and between the orbs of his buttocks.

Within minutes, the younger man was grunting and groaning and gasping as Zhukov, his gym shorts and jockstrap down around his ankles, worked his cock inside the younger man's passage. Patten cried out as Zhukov jerked his legs up and out, strong hands grasping the younger man's ankles, as he dove his cock deep into the channel and began to pump.

Patten panted and moaned, always surprised as how big the Russian was, how much deeper he could reach inside him than any other man, how vigorously the old man still could fuck him.

* * * *

"Are you sure you are staying here, that you aren't coming to the court?" Patricia Sebastian asked, more than a bit pissed, and her mood came across clearly. She was decked out to the nines in expensive-brand tennis wear, although she'd never lifted a racket herself and referred to the sets as innings, and had spent the entire morning getting her hair done, a manicure, and pedicure. She wanted to hear the commentators say that she and Stephanie looked more like sisters than mother and daughter.

"No, I'm sure. I'd be more of a nervous wreck than I am now," her husband, Andy, answered. He was sitting on the bed in shorts and a T-shirt. Open-toed sandals on his feet. He could have been going to a tennis match too, but one where he'd more likely be sitting in nose-bleed heaven than one of the players' boxes.

"This is your daughter's first super bowl final—maybe her last."

"It's a grand slam tennis event, Pat, not the super bowl. It being her first is all the more reason for me not to attend. I'd have a meltdown courtside whether she was winning or losing and the cameras would be delighted to catch that and take attention away from our daughter. All of the attention should be on her—speaking of which, you aren't really going to wear that hat in the player's box, are you?"

"Don't change the subject," Patricia said—although she took the neon-hued straw hat off and cast it on a chair, where, Andrew was later pleased to see, it was still pulsing when she'd left for the tennis venue. "It's just another example of you not supporting our daughter's career."

"That's not fair, Pat. I have worked my ass off to pay for her training and preparation and through two years of working her way into getting enough prize money to support herself. And I got her into Grigor Zhukov's tennis academy and moved my business down to Boca Raton so she'd have a house and family to come home to."

"And then moved the business back to Richmond after only two years. And left Stephanie and me alone down there for the next five years before she started into the junior tournaments."

"You don't understand, Pat. I did all I could. I was there when it mattered, and then I couldn't go on any . . ." He stopped. He hadn't told them before. He hadn't said anything to either Pat or Stephanie about it—ever. And today wasn't the day to bring it up. He had thought several times in the last three years that Pat knew something—but not that, not what was most significant and telling today—today of all days. Nothing had come up in the divorce, but he was sure that Pat had nosed out something. That's why he hadn't contested the divorce and had been generous. He no longer cared what Pat knew—but he didn't want Stephanie to know—or, god forbid, the press. Her career was just lifting to the pinnacle now. She didn't need any side circus attached to her.

"At least you'll be there afterward—for the parties and such—win or lose?"

"Yes, Pat. After the match—knowing its outcome one way or the other—I'll be there. Stephanie probably won't even know I wasn't in the stadium during any part of the match—unless you tell her, of course. We can tell everyone I just had to watch it from someplace inconspicuous, where the cameras couldn't pick me up."

"But you won't be there at all, will you?"

"No. I'll be here, in the hotel. Watching it on TV." And, in fact, Andrew planned on doing that—although not just that. But he had no intention of telling Pat what else he'd be doing. "And I have a strong feeling that those will be victory parties—victory parties for Stephanie—we'll be going to."

"You think so? Stephanie told me she wasn't sure at all. Maria Zhukov is a strong player, very strong. This isn't her first sup— . . . champion's final."

"Yes, but Maria doesn't have many more years in her and Stephanie is just coming up. I just have a strong feeling about this." The strong feeling was from inside track knowledge, although he'd never reveal it. And, though never mentioned, it was proof positive of what he'd do for Stephanie's career.

They left the room at the Sheraton LaGuardia East hotel together. It was Pat and Stephanie's room, not his. His room was three floors above. They no longer were a family, and Stephanie was nearly as dismissive of him now as Pat had been since the divorce. She too thought that he had deserted her. But she was as wrong as Pat about that.

He let Pat take the first elevator that responded, down to the ground floor and to the waiting limousine that would take her to Flushing Meadow and the limelight that she basked in—probably more so than Stephanie did. And then, with a deep sigh, he summoned another elevator to take him up three floors.

* * * *

Andrew had plenty of time to get back to his hotel room, take a long shower, and pad out into the room with just a towel around his waist and turn on the TV set to catch his daughter, looking younger than her twenty-one years and perky in a way that he knew meant she was a bundle of nerves, and Maria Zhukov, at thirty-two looking tough, determined, and "been here before" confident, come out of the tunnel and onto the court at Arthur Ashe Stadium. At nearly the same time as he switched on the TV set, there was a knock on his hotel room door.

"Did anyone see you?" he asked as he let the man into his room.

"No reporters, if that's what you mean," Grigor Zhukov answered. "But wouldn't that make the news: 'Dads fuck in Hotel Room while Daughters Battle at U.S. Open Final.'"

"That's not funny, Grigor," Andrew said, withdrawing into the room. Backing, whether he meant to or not to the edge of the bed, where Grigor advanced upon him, reaching out and placing the heel of his hand in the center of Andrew's chest.

"You've put on weight in last five years, Andy."

"Then perhaps you don't want to do this," Andrew snapped back.

"Not enough weight for me not to want to do this," Grigor snapped right back. "Have they started play yet?"

"You can see for yourself. The set's on. The girls are warming up."

"Good, we can fuck while they volley in first set. I can be there for trophy ceremony. Do you think I can time my thrusts with the rhythm of the volley?" He laughed at his own joke.

"Do you always have to be so crude—and so direct, Grigor?" Andrew asked.

"You always liked that about me. I don't pretend like you do."

"You *do* pretend, Grigor, or you'd be out of business."

"And you'd be out of a tennis star for a daughter. But enough of warm up for us." Grigor pushed Andrew down to a seated position on the bed with one hand and grabbed for and whipped off the towel Andrew had tied around his waist with the other hand. In short order, his own trousers and briefs had hit the floor, he had his hands cupping Andrew's ears, and he was guiding Andrew's mouth to his cock.

Andrew didn't fight him. He had known that Grigor was coming here. He had known what Grigor was coming for. He didn't go down on the cock immediately. His tongue went to the tight skin over Grigor's hairless groin and traced the line of a bluish vein down to the base of the cock and then down the cock. He was about to cover the oversized cap of the throbbing cock with his mouth, when, instead, he turned his face up to Grigor's.

"You did set it up, didn't you? I agreed to be here—for you, like this—because you were going to arrange for Stephanie to win. Maria has won two majors already. And she's thirty-two. You agreed that it was Stephanie's time, her turn. Right?"

Grigor laughed. "You would have been here for me even if I didn't . . . wouldn't you? No pretending." And then, when Andrew didn't answered, Grigor laughed again and said, "Suck me off. I don't have all day."

Andrew didn't have time to look at the set—or listen to the commentary—until Grigor had grabbed his knees and lifted and spread them so that he was digging his heels into the edge of the bed and had reclined back on the bed, holding Grigor's bald head between his hands and moaning as Grigor's mouth went down under his ball sac and the Russian's tongue darted between the crease of his buttocks.

Groaning and moaning deeply, Andrew turned his face to the TV set. The score was 3 to 1, first set, in Maria's favor. The camera went to the stands, picking out Maria's box and then Stephanie's, focusing in on Patricia preening for the camera, appearing not the least concerned that her daughter was down a break of serve, probably not even realizing that Stephanie already was losing.

Andrew shuddered and whimpered, his eye's slitting, "Please," he murmured.

"Please what?" Grigor queried, lifting his head, staring up along a naked, trembling torso that wasn't all that bad for a man of fifty.

"Please, if you're going to do it, get to it."

"You want cock, don't you? You're beginning to remember how much you wanted it; how often you begged for cock after first time I took you. I'm not here because of any deal you think you made for Stephanie, am I? I'm here because you remember cock and want it again. You never should have left Boca, left me."

Andrew groaned and turned his head toward the TV set. He didn't see it or hear it, though. He was thinking, thinking back to when Stephanie's talent was first remarked on. She was only six. It had taken nearly two years to get her into Zhukov's academy. Andrew had been thirty-four when he'd let the first man fuck him. He'd long fantasized about—and had been propositioned; he was quite a looker when younger—but he'd never been given enough of a reason to take the risk. Until he was trying to get Stephanie in the Zhukov academy. Zhukov, that first man, had been fifty-four. He told Andrew straight out what the conditions would be before he'd take Stephanie on as a student. He'd fucked Andrew for a year before she was permitted to enter the academy.

Five years ago, as Stephanie was showing the ability to move to the pros, Andrew had broken away. He left Boca Raton.

Moved his business back to Richmond. Left Patricia and Stephanie behind in Florida. Tried to celebrate his escape from Grigor. But he hadn't escaped, not really. There had been more men then. He ever had been on a quest for someone who could fuck him like Grigor had. The quest had not been fully successful. And then there had been the divorce.

The deal had been Grigor's idea, and Andrew had jumped to it—and, yes, damn it, it hadn't just been because of the deal. It had been because he never had gotten Grigor out of his system.

He cried out an "Oh, shit!" and clutched at the bedspread as Grigor entered him, strongly. And then he was panting and arching his back, putting his pelvis in motion, and gasping a litany of "Fuck me, fuck me, fuckmefuckme!" as Grigor thrust hard and deep and pistoned faster and faster until Andrew ejaculated up his belly and screamed a glorious release.

He lay back on the bed, exhausted, sweating, sighing, as Grigor stood between his thighs, still inside him, smiling, gripping his hips. Grigor slowly pulled out of him, pulled the condom off his cock, and commanded, "Make me come now." Andrew reached down, grabbed the big, hard cock in both hands, and began to stroke it.

"No, suck me off," Grigor said, moving up on the bed, his knees squeezing the sides of Andrew's chest, his torso leaning back, with his hands gripping Andrew's knees. He turned his head toward the TV set while Andrew closed his mouth over the cock and brought Grigor to an ejaculation.

Grigor brought his torso back up and looked down in Andrew's face. "You want me fuck you again, don't you?"

"Yes," Andrew answered. It was a reluctant yes, but it was a yes.

"You're sorry you ever left me, aren't you?"

"Yes," Andrew whispered. Grigor hadn't lost any of his virility in the past five years, any of his vigor, any of his stamina, any of his cock's ability to find and play every nook and cranny of Andrew's channel, deep. In Grigor's case, seventy wasn't old in every respect. Yes, damn it, yes Andrew wanted Grigor to fuck him again.

"Well, not now, I'm afraid. There isn't time now. But I'll be back tonight, after the parties. You'll be here, won't you?"

"Yes."

"And you got two key cards to the room, didn't you? You have one for me."

"Yes."

After Grigor had dressed and left the room, Andrew lay there for a few minutes, damning himself for his weakness—and for having already calculated how many hours he would have to endure until the parties were over and he was back in this room, waiting.

He heard the rise in applause on the television set and looked up in time to see that the set was over. Maria had won it 6 to 3. He sat, eyes plastered to the screen until it was all over. Grigor had made it to the tennis venue in time to be in his daughter's players' box to beam down at his daughter, Maria, as she climbed on a chair to receive victory hugs from those in her box.

The camera scanned to the other player's box. Patricia was still preening, probably oblivious to the fact that the match was over. Andrew had been right, though. If he'd been in that box when the camera scanned it, he wouldn't have been able to hide his disappointment.

Nobody knew what he'd had to do to enable Stephanie to get even this far. Nobody, of course, but Grigor Zhukov. And Grigor wouldn't see it as any sort of a sacrifice. Grigor considered himself to be a gift.

Andrew laughed. Who was he kidding? He saw Grigor as a gift too. And he knew there was no reason whatsoever to pretend with Grigor that there ever, really, had been any sort of a deal today that Andrew had consciously expected to be honored.

Screw Too Old

The Three Bitches, as a good many of the older ladies of the Summerside retirement community in Melbourne, Florida, referred to Annelise, Becky, and Karen, watched with barely suppressed sighs as new fellow resident, Phil, walked between their lounge beds and the edge of the community pool en route to the tennis courts. He did his best not to do more than nod, mumble "Ladies," and give a tight little smile. He knew that if he showed more interest than that the three would be on him like cats on a wounded sparrow, which he thought a particularly apt image.

"What a hunk," Becky muttered behind her Kindle after he'd walked by. "Have either of you . . . ?"

"Not me," Karen quickly answered.

"Me neither . . . not quite yet, although I think I might be getting somewhere with him," Annelise volunteered.

Annelise was ever the more optimistic and forward of the three, even though, at sixty-one, she was the oldest. She was the more manufacturedly perfect of the three, though, having had a fortune to spend on uplifts and tummy tucks and cosmetic miracles. The other two were not yet sixty, which made the three the youngest women in the community—and, thus, the disapproval gossip target of the other spinsters and widows who made up nearly 80 percent of the owners of manufactured homes surrounding the artificial finger lake of the community. The animosity went deeper than just their ages, though. The three hadn't given up yet. They hadn't given up on toning their bodies and beating off old age, and they hadn't given up on landing that last husband or sugar daddy. None of the three had given up on using the "fuck" word as more than just an explicative—or on doing it whenever they could maneuver a man who could get hard into their clutches.

Ever since Phil had moved in five weeks earlier, he had been the center of their attention as the newly minted most eligible man of the lot—this despite that he had recently hit seventy. It was a very well-preserved seventy, though, and neither of the Three Bitches were aware he was that old. He had always been a trim and handsome man who spent more than his share of time in the gym. And, as significant as anything else, thanks to his mother's genes, he'd kept a full head of hair that had turned a luminous shade of gray.

"You're putting us on about getting closer to him," Karen said, lowering her sunglasses to show Annelise that she was putting on a mock glower.

"If you think that then how would I know that he recently lost his wife? Her name was Lynn, she was younger than he is—about our age, which we should take as a sign, ladies—and he's devastated. It's not that he isn't interested, I'm sure. He's just still in shock and mourning."

"I wouldn't mind helping him get past mourning," Becky said, using a cooing voice tone. "He's one well-preserved man."

"He was a professional tennis player once, you know," Annelise said, determined to dole out the information she'd gleaned in the sales office slowly and with the inference she'd gotten it straight from him.

"Do tell?" Becky said. "His body certainly bears that out."

"Speaking of hunks," Karen muttered under her breath. "Look see who appeareth now. We're getting a parade of the best men in complex."

Heads swiveled as another man, in tennis togs, appeared from the same direction Phil had appeared and moved toward the same destination—the tennis court that adjoined the swimming pool. This man, Sergio, the recreation director of the community, was even hunkier than Phil was. Of course he was twenty years younger than Phil was. A Brazilian, with an accent that the women of the community swooned over, Sergio was all muscle—for his age—and deeply tanned.

The Three Bitches adjusted their lounge beds slightly to get a better view of the tennis courts, and they swooned and sighed in unison as both men took off their shirts and moved to opposite sides of the court to start warming up.

"Oh, god, what I'd give to be fucked by that Brazilian," Becky cooed.

"I'd happily open my legs for either one of them," Karen chimed in.

"Best concentrate on Phil," Annelise said with a knowing smirk, "Sergio wouldn't be interested."

"Oh, how would you know that?" Karen challenged her. "Lots of men wear an earring like that—although I'm a little leery of the nipple ring. But if you ask me, it's very sexy. In fact, they're both very sexy. I'm melting."

"You've been out in this sun too long. You're beginning to take on the cast of old leather." Becky turned back to Annelise then. "You know that because you hit on him and he didn't bite? Not every man who's straight will want to get into your bikini bottoms, Little Miss Perfect."

"I know what I know," Annelise persisted.

"I still say I'd open my legs for either one of them," Karen said in a dreamy voice, her eyes plastered on the tennis court, her attention bouncing back and forth between the two shirtless men along with the movement of the tennis ball.

* * * *

"You let me win," Sergio said when he and Phil had finished their match on the tennis court and were swigging bottled water by the bench where they had stashed their gear. "With what I'd heard about you having been on the pro circuit, I thought I didn't have a chance."

"The pro circuit was decades ago, Sergio," Phil answered. "I'm just an old man today. I ran out of steam, and you're a much younger man. And you play very well too." Phil was rotating an arm at the shoulder and wincing a bit, not yet stowing his gear away as Sergio was busy doing.

"I'm not a young man either," Sergio said with a laugh.

"Twenty years or so, I'd say," Phil countered. "It makes a difference."

"Not twenty years, surely" Sergio said, with a laugh, but happy that Phil seemed to think he was about forty. "I'm fifty, and you're probably the most fit sixty-year-old in the community."

"Seventy," Phil interjected.

Sergio whistled appreciatively. "I would never have guessed," he said, "and I can see why I won the match now. You're having trouble with those shoulder muscles, aren't you?"

"It's what age—and inactivity—will do for you," Phil answered, the tone of regret and defeat coming through loud and clear in his voice.

Sergio gave him a sharp look and then turned and finished stowing his gear away. "I promised I'd come by and help you get your computer hooked up," he said, not looking at Phil, who was still looking dejected as he pulled a Polo shirt over his torso and starting putting his tennis stuff in his bag. "Any time convenient for you that I can come over to do that?"

"Sure, any time you can schedule it," Phil answered, his voice flat. And then he continued in a somewhat faraway voice, "Any time at all. I'm not going anywhere . . . any more. I have all the time in the world now."

"How about tomorrow afternoon at 4:00 p.m.? I have an exercise class to give at 2:00. I'd have plenty of time to wrap that up and get showered."

"4:00 it is then," Phil said as he turned to walk away. "And . . . thanks for helping with the computer. I'm a dunce at that. It was always taken care of by . . . let's just say that anything electronic is way beyond me. And thanks for the tennis game too. I'd gotten rusty."

"I'm the one who should thank you for the tennis. Now I can say I've played a pro—and I'm willing to bet this is the last time I win. And the help with the computer is just one of my jobs here. Happy to do it." Sergio didn't turn to watch Phil depart until Phil was almost at the gate in the tall, chain-link fence surrounding the tennis court. Phil hesitated, perhaps thinking of turning to say something, but then he resumed moving through the gate and toward the swimming pool, his body in a stance of dejection.

Sergio had meant this tennis game to be something to lift the new resident's spirits. As soon as he'd heard that Phil had been a professional tennis player when he was younger, Sergio had thought this would be a way to help the man settle in at Summerside. Many coming here as their first stop in a retirement community had trouble adjusting to the life. And it was part of Sergio's job, as the recreational director, to do what he could to get them settled in. Phil was more forlorn and withdrawn than most. Of course, Sergio had been told that Phil was here because he was recently widowed and had had a spouse who did almost everything for him.

Such residents usually were the toughest ones to fit in.

Beyond doing his duty, Sergio was attracted to Phil. Really good-looking man, Sergio thought. There's no way he would have guessed Phil had hit seventy. He had kept himself in great shape— probably a function of having been a professional athlete—and he was quite a handsome man. Yes, quite a handsome man indeed, Sergio thought.

The Three Bitches interrupted their chattering as Karen noticed that the tennis game was over and Phil was walking by between them and the side of the pool again. She nudged the other two and they went into a "we don't notice you at all, we don't even see you" pose as they scrutinized Phil's progress behind Kindles and magazines across their field of sight.

"He looks sad," Becky whispered.

"I'd still jump his bones in a nanosecond," Karen whispered back.

"He's well worth it," Annelise said smugly. "He's hung."

"You've never," Becky hissed. "You're just putting us on."

"You just don't know how to interpret sweaty tennis shorts," Annelise answered with a sniff in her voice.

The three giggled into their tanned, manicured hands. Phil just kept on walking, not looking around, although the giggles were loud enough to reach his ears. He had no time for the women of the Summerside retirement community—to him, the last stop in this life—and, considering the depth of the grief of his recent loss, his stay here couldn't possibly be too short.

* * * *

"The computer is in the bedroom," Phil said when he opened the door to Sergio the next afternoon. "And thanks for doing this. I know that if I tried to hook it up, I'd blow the electricity for the entire community. I'll go make us some coffee. I think staying out of the way would be my best contribution to this."

"You might be right," Sergio said as he entered the manufactured home, "there are some people who are quite talented otherwise who just don't seem to be able to get along with electronics."

"That would be me," Phil answered, moving toward the kitchen at the right, as Sergio headed toward the door to the master bedroom to the left. "I had someone to take care of all of that for me. I had Lynn."

Was that a catch in Phil's voice Sergio heard? He kept his eyes turned away from Phil and toward his destination, the master bedroom. This was a retirement community he was working in. He was accustomed to the older folks coming here not long after the loss of their spouse—or not long before they themselves passed on. It wasn't just any depression they might feel from moving from a substantial suburban home to what, essentially, was a glorified trailer park. It was too much change too late in life—an awareness that life had passed them by.

Sergio couldn't see the housing units here as anything but fancy trailers. Once inside Phil's unit, though, he could see that it was as solid looking as any stick-built home. But if you looked carefully you could see that the walls weren't wood or brick but some other man-made board covered in vinyl wallpaper. The interior was commodious enough, for one person, with the hub of the building being a kitchen-dining area-family room section, with a large master bedroom and bath and a smaller guest room and main bathroom off the family room. To the right, beyond the kitchen and dining areas was a large living room, which looked like it was used mainly as a transit room to a screened porch, facing the lake. Phil had managed to snarf up one of the premium lots right on the water.

Phil himself looked in better spirits today than yesterday. And to Sergio he looked good—trim, but well muscled, still causing Sergio to disbelieve that the man was seventy. He still had a full head of hair, which always helped to keep a man looking younger, even though it had gone fully to gray. He was wearing a close-fitting white T-shirt over white shorts today, which contrasted nicely with the tan he was developing. He might have lost steam on the tennis court yesterday, Sergio thought, and left dejected for some reason, but exercising out in the sun was benefiting him—and making him look hot to someone like Sergio in more ways than temperature.

The computer desk was set in the corner of what was a pretty large bedroom, dominated by a queen-sized bed. All the modules needed were there, but Sergio could tell from the tangle of wires that Phil had made a half-hearted effort to hook it up himself but had stopped quickly in frustration. Computer support was key to Sergio's recreation services job, though, so he had no trouble seeing what needed to be done and getting down to doing it.

There was a shelf above the computer desk. A few books laying on their backs and stacked on top of each other, but there were photographs too—of Phil, some younger, some recent—and also of who must be Lynn. Sergio did a double take at seeing the photos and began to readjust his thinking about Phil—and his own attitude toward Phil.

Phil had arrived with a cup of coffee for Sergio. "Is it a hopeless mess?" he asked.

"Not at all," Sergio answered. "We should have you up and running in no time."

"Thanks," Phil said. Sergio was looking up at him and saw Phil wince. The older man put his own cup of coffee down on the top of a nearby bureau and rotated the same arm he was having trouble with at the close of the match the previous day. The expression on his face showed that he was in some pain.

"Your shoulder. It's still hurting you?"

"Yes, a little. Just getting to be too old for tennis. Too old for much of anything."

"Nonsense. You're too good a player to give it up this young. You've kept in great shape. A massage could take care of that."

"I suppose," Phil answered noncommittally. He picked up his coffee cup and turned to leave. "You'll do better without me to jinx the computer build," he said. "Trust me on that. I'll be in the other room, marinating a steak for dinner."

"I see you have photographs," Sergio said, arresting Phil's departure. "You and Lynn, I take it?"

Phil's gaze went to the photographs as if seeing them for the first time, just now realizing he'd left them there. There was a nervous pause and then he sighed and said, "Yes, that's us. That's Lynn. Much younger than me. It should have been me who went first."

"I understand," Sergio said, saying so much in that phrase, saying enough to be able to see some of the tension draining out of Phil that had suddenly arisen at the realization that he hadn't put those photographs away before Sergio arrived.

"I'll . . . I'll be in the kitchen if there's anything you're missing here that I might be able to find for you."

"I don't think I'm missing anything," Sergio said. "Everything's fine. I mean it, Phil. Everything's fine."

Phil gave him a look with a touch of surprise in it and then left the room.

After he got the computer going and hooked up to the Internet, Sergio tested the machine out on some of his own favorite Web sites—just to be sure. And when he found that everything was as he expected, everything was fine.

"So, how did it go?" Phil asked, as Sergio came out of the bedroom. "Find everything you needed?"

"Yes, thanks, I found out all I needed to know. And you're good to go now."

He had taken his time. He could see, looking the full length of the home to the bay window in the living room opening to a lake view, that twilight was beginning to descend. While he'd been working on the computer, he'd decided that he'd like it to be close to dinnertime before he finished.

"What do I owe you?" Phil asked. "You're a lifesaver. A guy can't be without the Internet—even an old guy like me. Especially an old guy like me—suddenly living alone."

"You don't owe me anything. It's part of my job. But I would have been happy to have done it for you anyway."

"Well, we're well into happy hour," Phil said, after a pause during which Sergio hadn't moved toward the front door. "How about a drink out on the screen porch before you go? Although it seems you deserve more than that for getting me hooked up."

"A drink would be nice, thanks. And, well, if it's not asking too much, I see that you have two steaks marinating there. I live alone myself . . . and it's getting toward supper time . . ."

"Yes, of course. I should have invited you myself. I haven't been too swift lately in my thinking. Let's have the drink—or maybe a couple—out on the screened porch and then I'll put the steaks on. We can eat on the porch too. I spend a lot of time out there—alone—watching the lake. Getting this lot was the best decision I made in moving here."

They had two drinks before Phil put the steaks on, and the conversation had become loose and warm as they watched the sun sink over the lake. Phil obviously hadn't had anyone to talk to for some time, and Sergio studiously was being the good listener. There still were areas, facets of Phil's life, that he didn't go into, but Sergio was being very open about his own life—and his preferences.

He wanted Phil to know.

As they were finishing their steaks, Sergio brought up Phil's problem with his shoulder again. He obviously was in pain even from the slightest use of it while setting up and breaking down the supper elements. "I think that a massage would do that a world of good. I don't want you to stop playing tennis. I want to play more with you myself."

"I suppose. I guess I could check around to see—"

"I'm a trained masseur. I could take care of that for you myself."

"You could?" Phil's expression was one of surprise, as if he'd never considered this before and that it was significant information.

Sergio put his drink down and turned serious eyes on Phil. "Yes. I can help you. I want to help you."

The seriousness of Sergio's expression wasn't lost on Phil. They'd been dancing around the topic for a couple of hours now, honing ever closer to the center of the issue, and Phil had made no suggestion that it was time for Sergio to leave. "I'm an old man, Sergio. I'm past all that. But thanks for the offer."

"Screw the old man stuff," Sergio spat out. "You are only as old as you want to be. I can give you a good massage, a special massage. I want to."

"Here, now?" Phil said, a note of panic in his voice.

"No, not tonight. We're both liquored up tonight. I wouldn't want any part of my massage to hurt you or be what you didn't want. I'll be back tomorrow, same time. That will give you plenty of time to decide whether you want a massage. If not, though, it isn't because you are an old man and can't take the sort of massage that would do you good."

* * * *

"God, you're as good as Lynn. You're better than Lynn," Phil gasped. He was lying, face down on a portable massage table in the middle of his living room, naked other than a towel draped over his buttocks. Sergio, stripped to the waist, was standing above him, working Phil's shoulder muscles with a deep-tissue massage.

"Lynn gave you massages then, did he?" Sergio asked in low, thick voice. He still couldn't believe that Phil was seventy. He had the body of a much younger man. He was thickening, yes, but he was still solid and had muscle tone.

"Yes, Lynn did everything for me. Lynn was everything for and to me."

"I can't replace Lynn; I don't want to replace him," Sergio answered—he, in fact, thought he could replace Phil's younger, male lover, and he wanted to, but this wasn't the time to assert that—"but I can give you massages. And," he boldly added, "I could give you so much more."

Surely Phil wasn't so slow on the uptake not to know what Sergio was offering, the Brazilian thought. If Phil was going to reject the offer, this is where it should occur.

They continued in silence for a while, as Phil grunted, groaned, and moaned to the deep-healing touch of Sergio's hands on his body. Sergio slowly worked his way down Phil's torso, taking and massaging each extremity, in turn, and then working the muscles in the small of Phil's back. Pushing the towel down onto Phil's calves and working his glutes. Massaging his butt cheeks and squeezing and separating them. Letting the edge of his hands rub across Phil's ass entrance. Listening for either a tightening and a voiced rejection or a sighing and spreading of Phil's legs by his own actions.

There was an initial tightening, but then, slowly, a relaxation, a sigh, and a low sob. Sergio could feel the tension going out of Phil's buttocks, and Phil parted his thighs. Sergio allowed the tips of his fingers to play along the opening in the crease between the butt cheeks. By the time the greased fingers had entered Phil's channel, Phil had turned his head and accepted Sergio's hard cock in his mouth, Sergio having somehow lost his sweatpants in the process and now being as naked as Phil was.

Sergio coaxed Phil to raise his pelvis a bit while Sergio's cock moved in and out of Phil's mouth. The younger Brazilian moved a hand between Phil's thighs and pulled the older man's cock and balls through and started to pull on and gently squeeze the balls while fisting and then stroking Phil's engorging cock with his hand.

Phil moaned and, letting Sergio's hard cock fall out of his mouth momentarily, whispered something that Sergio was assured was encouragement and an acceptance.

"I want to fuck you," Sergio murmured.

In answer, Phil took the cock back into his mouth.

There was no longer any question what Phil preferred in sex—that it had been a younger male lover who had taken good care of Phil's needs, but who had died before his time—whose

90

death had convinced Phil that his own life was also over and had motivated him to move to a retirement community to slowly fade away.

Sergio was showing him that he wasn't really ready to fade away yet. That there were men—Sergio foremost among them—who could still find Phil desirable and who would like to give him what he needed.

Sergio climbed up on the table, straddling Phil's hips.

He covered Phil close for a moment, murmuring in his ear, "I'm going to fuck you now."

The only response he got from Phil was a low moan. But the older man cried out in surprise and wonder and ecstasy as Sergio's cock entered his channel. His head raised to where he could see the sun shimmering on the lake through the living room bay window, as Sergio began to stroke inside him. Without losing the rhythm of the stroke, Sergio leaned his torso over Phil's back, grabbed Phil's biceps to hold him down on the table, and began to stroke faster and deeper.

"Oh, god. Oh shit. I never thought . . . again . . . ever," Phil cried out.

Sergio lowered his lips to Phil's ear, kissed his earlobe, ran his tongue into the ear canal, and then whispered, "Never say you're too old. As long as you can take this, as long as you want it, never say you're too old to fuck. I want you, and I'll fuck you like this whenever you want me. Neither one of us is too old to take our pleasure with each other."

"Look at him. Head held high, very nice chest stuck out, looking like he'd swallowed a canary."

Becky had spoken to her Three Bitches cohorts from their usual station, parked at the side of the swimming pool on lounge beds in bikinis that had been destined for much younger women. Karen and Annelise looked up to see that Phil was strutting past them, all smiles, on his way to meet Sergio at the tennis court. He was shirtless and looking mighty fine for a man even ten years younger than he was.

"Yes, I can tell someone got to him and made him happy to be here. Some woman has managed to get into his pants and bed."

Karen and Becky turned to Annelise, who was humming but who wasn't saying anything, just smiling a smug smile.

"You?" Karen accused. "For real?"

"We should have known," Becky chimed in.

Let them think what they want, Annelise mused. I haven't said yes. The evasion is worth them thinking I'm one up on them.

"That leaves Sergio," Becky said, with a sigh, turning her head to the tennis court, where the two men were chattering and laughing, as they moved to opposite sides of the court. "I wouldn't say he's second best."

"But I'd say he's well beyond the charms of any of us," Annelise said. "He looks like he's getting it too, but, from what I hear, it isn't from the likes of any of us. Pity. Such a waste of manflesh."

As the two men started to volley the tennis ball back and forth, Phil admired the physique of the man across from the net from him, his mind going to how his hands had moved over the hard muscles of the Brazilian's body the previous night as Sergio covered him closely and Phil opened his legs to the insistent cock. Who would have known Sergio, at his age, had the stamina to fuck him three times during the night? Phil smiled broadly, feeling twenty years younger, as he dove for a ball. He could have vouched for both Becky's belief that Sergio was "getting it" and Annelise's reply that it wasn't from the likes of the Three Bitches. He could also attest that Sergio wasn't a waste of manflesh. No, not at all.

Tempting Memory

Jude had gotten through the second set at The Spot in Chelsea the same way he had gotten through all of Logjam's concerts in the last two decades—riding a high on the music, the roar of the crowd, beer, and poppers. If the proportion of beer and poppers had been relentlessly creeping up over the last fifteen years, it had been too gradual for Jude to notice it, or too scary for him to acknowledge it.

Logjam was still a big-name rock band—well, a relatively big name. Other bands still played its covers from the eighties. And the band still got regular concert gigs even if their range was narrowing down to between Boston to the north and Philadelphia to the south and increasingly was one-night club stands like here at The Spot more than playing—as opening acts more now than headlining—in stadium venues.

Jude Crown, on electric guitar and occasional backup vocals, was one of three original members of Logjam, which gave him a big say in what the band did—and being "in" with the promoter gave him an even bigger say. However, it also meant that he was fifty years old. He did everything he could to remain "hip"— long hair. dyed blond now rather than its original golden sheen; a signature red bandana and torn jeans; muscle shirts, and the constant working out to make wearing one plausible; and tattoos. But he also relied on no longer being a front man on stage, but gyrating at the edge of the shadows now.

And being able to stay upright throughout a concert was taking more poppers and beer now than it had ten years ago. He might have given the perpetual gig up, as three of the original band members had—two of them twenty years ago—if his financial decisions had been as good as theirs had been, and if he didn't live for the roar of the crowd.

The crowd still roared for him. Young women still flipped their bras and panties over the footlights for him, as young men— more in the know than the women—did with their bikini briefs. If it hadn't been for this, he would have retreated some time ago, remained at home with Bronson, and faded into old age.

The crowd worship was no different tonight. But more telling was the interest expressed by the drummer from one of the other bands playing The Spot this evening, a near-boy band of rich young blond guys—guys much as Logjam had been when they first came together, other than the rich part. As Jude had played in Logjam's sets, the drummer from the younger band, none of its members much over twenty, had stood, just in the shadow of the stage wings, near where Jude was doing his thing steaming up his guitar and gyrating his hips to the music. Jude could see the young guy from the corner of his eye. He was hanging on every note Jude snatched from his guitar and every move of Jude's hips. Jude felt like he was being undressed onstage. He wasn't surprised; he had heard guarded and snide comments about the sexual proclivities of the members of this younger band.

The blond drummer was smoking a joint—against all rules about fire on the stage, even here in this "regulations are to be pissed off" hard rock music venue. As Jude brushed by him in the close confines of flying side curtains leading into the stage, the drummer reached out and laid a hand on Jude's arm, smiled at him, and offered him a drag on the joint.

Jude smiled back, and accepted the joint. The drummer said something, but the next band was already revving up on stage at a decibel level that jerked the young blond's words away.

"What's that?" Jude said, returning the joint and making an "I can't hear you" gesture with his hand and his facial expressions.

The drummer pulled Jude close to him and nearly screamed in his ear, "I've followed you for like, ever, man. You really send me. I'd like to get it on with you, man. I've heard what you like."

Jude nodded dumbly at him, his mind taking a few extra seconds to recheck what words he'd actually said and to analyze them. He was flattered, of course. The guy probably was a few months shy of twenty, and he was a real hunk. It hit Jude that what he was wearing mimicked what Jude himself was wearing—his signature look—and so maybe the kid wasn't putting him on about following his career. But he couldn't have followed more than half of Jude's career. He wasn't old enough to have done that.

That a young guy like this was hitting on him was more of a high for Jude than the beer, poppers, and proffered joint combined. Jude's sex life had been a bit skittish the last few months. "Get it on," he'd said. Jude knew what that meant in this context. He was fifty and some stud of a kid still wanted to get it on with him.

"I don't know," screamed back in the drummer's ear. "You got another set? Time's rollin' on."

"Naw, I'm finished. I'm told Logjam is finished for the night too. But the night's young. There's another club." He named the club, which Jude knew was a gay bar a dozen blocks away. "And I thought . . . maybe . . . my place afterward. It's close. It's private."

Figures, Jude thought. He'd heard these dudes were from rich families. The drummer apparently had an apartment—probably even a loft apartment—of his own—in New York City.

The loudness of the music on the stage, and stagehands trying to muscle around them to take additional equipment out onto the stage as one band segued into the next, had caused the two men to become plastered together closely so that they could hear each other. The drummer handed his joint over again, and while that hand was free, he used it to fondle Jude's basket through the worn denim of the jeans and then to snake the hand around Jude's back and squeeze one of his butt cheeks and maintain a hold there.

The signaling was obvious. But the drummer made it more obvious, leaning into Jude's ear and saying, "I give great head; no one's complained about it. And I hear you like to take big cock. I can handle that."

"I don't know, maybe," Jude answered, clearly flattered and getting aroused. Jude's main question was answered, though. The guy was young, and Jude had been afraid that he wanted to be spiked. But he obviously knew that that was what Jude liked himself and was still making the offer. "I'd have to meet you there, though—at that club. And a little later. Something I'd got to do first."

"No problem," the drummer said. "You're call, man." He took a pen out of the pocket of his tight, worn jeans; took hold of Jude's forearm; turned it to the underside, which was free of hair and tattoos; and wrote the name and street of the bar and his cell phone number on the skin of Jude's arm. "Don't be long; I can show you a real good time."

Jude watched the young guy turn and disappear into the pall of smoke, a mix of forbidden cigarette smoke and the overdemand of the night's bands for stage smoke.

At the drummer's urging, Jude had copped a feel of the guy's package himself and had shuddered from the feel of the size of him. It would be a real romp of a night, he could tell. The dude was hung and young and he sashayed his butt as he floated off.

The glitch—why Jude couldn't just leave with him, not let the kid out of his sight until after they'd fucked, not give the guy time to register that Jude was fifty and the kid was shy of twenty—was Bronson. He was back at their apartment. He hadn't felt well, he'd said, when Jude was getting ready to come down to The Spot, and Jude had promised to at least check in with him after his sets here were finished. Bronson was good with Jude barhopping after giving a concert in the city, but Jude didn't know what he'd think of what the drummer had offered.

The age difference between the drummer and Jude was even greater than that between Jude and Bronson, who was seventy now. The two of them had been together for over thirty years, though. Would the young drummer still hit on Jude if he thought ahead on a prospect of an age difference like that between Jude and Bronson, the electric guitarist wondered.

Probably not. And if Jude didn't want the young guy to start thinking about it, it had better be a brief check on Bronson at the apartment before Jude got his ass over to that gay bar. He hadn't had any in weeks now, and that made him jittery.

* * * *

Jude laid his head back on the top edge of the backseat of the taxi as it drove him back to the apartment he shared with Bronson—or, rather, the apartment Bronson had bought in their heyday and Jude occupied with him. He needed to clear his head a bit of the drugs and beer high if he was going to fully appreciate the sex with the young hunk. He was in the taxi not only because who needed a car—or could find a parking spot for it—in New York City but also because he didn't have his license. He had a license; he'd kept up the one from West Virginia. It just had been suspended for the third time for drunken drives he'd made home in Bronson's car from gigs in Boston or Philadelphia.

Bronson had bailed him out each time, and losing the licenses was no big deal as long as the out-of-town concerts were thinning out, which they were. Other than that nuisance, the brushes with the law were actually beneficial to business. Each time he lost his license or got into some sort of brawl, there'd be a snippet in the newspaper on his latest bad-boy behavior. There was no better assurance than that that he hadn't fully sunk into oblivion. His police blotter still was worth an inch and a half in the newspaper. It still was good publicity.

The poppers, the beer, and the exhaustion from the two vigorous hard rock sets—at his age—all contributing, Jude drifted into a haze of reverie. Cute young guy. Jude was that at one time too. Promise of a big cock and a good fuck. Bronson had the biggest cock—and gave the best fuck—that Jude could remember—in his prime. The gay bar wasn't that far from Bronson's apartment . . . maybe wouldn't need a taxi . . .

He'd thought his first band was really good—that they'd go far. At the time, though, Jude wasn't looking any farther than Charleston, West Virginia. And, in retrospect, the band sucked and probably wouldn't have gotten any farther than Charleston if it had stayed together. He'd been pretty good, though. Bronson had agreed with him on that. Bronson wasn't just interested in him to get some young tail, although Jude has thought at first that was all it was.

Jude's band—he was the lead—had been playing a road house on the cheap edge of Charleston and Bronson had been driving back to New York City from Nashville. He'd stopped at the roadhouse for a beer and stayed to listen to the band—to Jude, specifically, who already was very good on the guitar and not bad as the band's lead singer. And he was a beautiful young blond, just the sort of young man Bronson liked to debauch.

And debauch Jude he had. Jude had played around with guys before. He had played with young women too. For southern West Virginia, he was a stand-out gorgeous hunk and knew it. He could have anyone he wanted—the bored, underemployed young people in the area worshiped the bands no matter how crummy they played. And Jude didn't play crummy, not even then, pretty much at the beginning. He radiated beauty and happiness and just loving life. The women he fucked; the guys—mostly hunky miners or mine owners who could spot him a steak dinner—fucked him.

Bronson fucked him. Repeatedly through the night in a nearby motel. He pitched Jude with the "I'm a music producer and promoter, you're something special, and I can make you a star" routine to get Jude into the sack. Despite the business cards, Jude didn't believe Bronson. He'd gotten that line before—even the fake business cards. But Bronson looked good, even though he was twenty years older than Jude, and there was that steak dinner, and the motel looked less seedy than where Jude had planned to go back to that night.

And then they were in the motel room, and Bronson was sucking him off—expertly. And manhandling Jude to suck him off, which impressed Jude. He liked to be manhandled. And then, Jude on his back and his legs raised and spread, Bronson was pistoning him with a long, thick cock that knew just how to play Jude's channel right. And then he was fucking him doggy style on the bed, and then he was fucking him from behind in the shower, and then he dragged him out of the shower and carried Jude to the bed, slapped him down on his back, wishboned his legs and . . .

It had gone on all night, and Jude had loved the attention and the biggest, most vigorous cock he'd ever taken.

And in the morning, he was surprised to see Bronson still there in bed with him, and then to feel Bronson roll over on top of him and spread his legs, enter him again, and make him pant and moan and rake his fingernails on Bronson's shoulder blades, and arch his back and cry out his ejaculation as Bronson's cock continued to churn inside him.

More surprising than that was that Bronson took him to breakfast and told him he could make him a star and offered to drive him to New York and give him a place to stay and food to eat while Jude became established in the rock band world. Jude had reckoned that Bronson would take him as far as Harrisonburg over in Virginia and would fuck him all night in another motel and then would abandon him, but Jude didn't particularly care. He'd never been outside of West Virginia, there wasn't anything important on his social schedule for the next few days, and Bronson had a cock to die for.

Imagine his surprise when Bronson took him all the way to New York City—although the night-long cocking in motels had continued—and did, indeed, give him a side of his bed and provided food, although Jude had to do more than his share of preparing it, *and* established that his business card announcing him as a music producer and promoter wasn't a fake—nor was he small time at what he did.

Over the next thirty years, Bronson did everything for Jude. He got him matched with a band, whose members were all better than he was but were willing to help him grow into his own significant talent. Bronson had provided the Logjam name, correctly identified winning tunes coming from within the band and supplied winning tunes from the outside to complement those, got the band increasingly better gigs, managed Jude's finances—to the extent he could; Jude's ability to let money slip through his fingers in nondurable goods and services was his talent alone—and, when the band was over their pinnacle and on the way down, had made sure that the drop was slow and comfortable and that they continued to have a reputation that was recalled and respected.

It had only been in the last couple of months that Bronson had been failing, had been leaving Jude at loose ends and with some idea that the ride wouldn't last—a ride that had already lasted for thirty years.

And hadn't been riding Jude.

"We're here . . . sir," the taxi driver announced over his shoulder, obviously a bit confused on whether a fifty-year-old guy dressed as a rocker should be addressed as sir.

Jude looked through the window of the cab, the world beyond the window still a bit foggy in his brain, although he was beginning to sober up. He was home. Not his home, of course. This continued to be Bronson's apartment house. Nice enough, but nothing fancy. Bronson had put all of his eggs in the Logjam basket, and as they started down the other side of the peak of success, his fortunes had slid a bit too. For thirty years, everything that he had and was able to do had been invested in Jude.

And the sex had been good that long—well, almost that long. Bronson always seemed tired now. Jude had always come home for the cock. He was home again. He turned his arm to where he could see the forearm and the address and telephone number written on it in ink. He could feel his cock harden. The young blond was fresh, a new, big cock. Jude could still feel the sensation of running his hand over the length of the young drummer's cock through the tight material of the guy's jeans. Jude was in heat. A real groupie for Jude, not just in what he said and offered, but because he had mimicked Jude's signature look. He'd give Jude everything Jude wanted. Bronson hadn't . . . not for weeks.

"This is the right address, isn't it . . . sir?" the taxi driver's voice cut into Jude's reverie.

"Yeah, yeah. This is home."

* * * *

Jude entered the bedroom quietly. He found himself listening for breathing. It was much too soon to be worried about that, of course, but he'd started listening for such things and emotionally withdrawing the moment Bronson had told him what was wrong, why he'd been listless lately.

Bronson was lying on his back on the bed, naked, the sheet kicked off him. A fever had probably come and gone sometime while Jude was gone, but the sheets appeared dry. Jude wouldn't have to change them before he left. Light from the street below filtered in through the window, not now covered with drapes. It was dim but not totally dark in the room. Just the right light to be kind to Bronson's body. He hadn't started wasting away yet—not noticeably—and in the dim light he looked a lot younger than his seventy years. Still a handsome man. Still a good body. And most certainly still a long, thick cock, even in repose.

Jude stripped down and went to the bathroom and took a shower. A two-set rock concert under hot lights was sweaty work—especially for a fifty-year-old like him. All the clothes he'd worn tonight would have to go into the hamper. While he showered, he went through the ritual of cleaning himself out and went hard, thinking of the blond drummer and what he promised. To a guy Jude's age, such a promise couldn't be considered lightly.

He toweled himself off as he came back into the room. Bronson hadn't moved. God, he looks good—still—in this light, Jude thought. He went to the bureau and opened a drawer, looking for bikini briefs. Deciding against briefs—he'd feel sexier in the getting-better-acquainted period in the bar before the blond took him home and fucked him—Jude opened another drawer where he kept his tight T's. He'd kept himself in good shape. He wanted the drummer to see and appreciate that. His eyes fell on the document on top of the dresser. The papers on his bail bond for his most-recent DUI charge.

He'd been in Trenton, New Jersey, on his way home from a gig in Philadelphia. It was 3:30 a.m., and not the best place, in terms of cop consideration, to be drunk at 3:30 a.m. and thrown in the slammer. He hadn't thought twice about who to call. Bronson had come immediately. Hadn't even asked about his car that Jude had been driving. He just wanted to know how Jude was and how much money would be needed. And this was the third time. Bronson had looked like death warmed over when he arrived in Trenton, driven by one of the other band members in that guy's car. It only occurred to Jude now that Bronson had just been coming off a chemo treatment then. He couldn't have driven himself even if it hadn't been his car that Jude had been driving. But he came immediately when Jude needed him.

Bronson snorted over in the bed, and, hearing him, Jude turned and went over and sat on the bed beside the older man. His hand, by habit, went to Bronson's cock and he began to stroke it. Bronson stirred and opened his eyes. He smiled at Jude.

"How did it go?" He was asking about the concert, but for a brief, panicked moment, Jude got the idea he was asking about the hookup offer. He felt embarrassed.

"Good as always. We still have it."

"*You* still have it. Some of the newer members of the band aren't up to snuff. I'll be looking for a better drummer."

The word "drummer" made Jude wince. And here Bronson, with this pressing problem of his own, was still thinking of the band, thinking of Jude's needs.

Jude leaned over, took the engorging cock in his mouth, and gave it mouth play. Bronson sighed and held Jude's head between his hands, moving his fingers through Jude's hair, and helping the head move up and down on the cock.

He can still get it up, Jude thought. He can still get it up for me. After thirty years. Just two old dudes growing old together. He pulled off the cock, lifted his face to Bronson's, and the two kissed deeply, fitting together perfectly, their tongues doing what they'd done for thirty years.

Jude pulled away, and stood up from the bed, letting loose of the cock that, now, was everything that Jude had ever wanted, could ever want. "Just a minute. I have to take a piss." He padded, naked, back into the bathroom and did take a piss. But when he turned to the wash basin and after he washed his hands, he also kept the soap, reached for the washcloth, and rubbed soap and water into the lower side of his forearm until the address and telephone number that had been written there was completely obliterated.

Returning to the bedroom, he mounted the bed and straddled Bronson's pelvis, reaching back to grasp the older man's still-hard cock, and beginning to descend his channel on the shaft. "I know you're tired," he whispered. "I'll do the riding this time. But I'll want it again afterward—just like old times. If you think you can . . ."

"Of course I can. I'll always take care of you." Bronson sighed and his gnarled hands latched onto Jude's waist, doing what he could to help Jude rise and fall on the cock. "Yes, just like old times. Forever and ever."

No matter how long forever lasts, Jude thought.

Tuscan Memory

The letter both disturbed me and drew me to it, time and time again. It said so little, but there was so much there between the lines. I wasn't the only one who went on with life after that summer—and yet there was the hint of something more, perhaps the yearning for another act, not just the memory of what was meant to be a final curtain.

What had happened in the life of the other? And why this letter? Just a note really, not saying anything really. But why a letter at all, after this many years? Why open old wounds, old yearnings? I felt all of my seventy years. I couldn't just sit here and dwell on the letter, unfold it and read it again and again. I had to do something—be up and moving around—something to keep me from feeling so, so old. I must cast the letter aside and do something else to regain the younger me I didn't want to let loose of, as best I could.

As I sat at the writing desk in my bed chamber, I gazed out of the window looking down the slope of Tuscan vineyards. My grandson, sweet Paulo, was working in the vineyard, stripped down to the waist, strongly, beautifully built, looking, I'm sure, how I looked as a youth—how Daniel looked that summer. I sighed, closed the lid of the secretary on the burning presence of the folded letter, tucked away now in a secret compartment, and rose from the desk. I couldn't just sit here like this, trying to avoid memories I had done everything I could to lock up in the back of my mind. I had to do something to not feel quite so . . . old. I decided that a trip to the spa was in order

As always, a trip to the hot spa and springs at Val d'Orcia had made me feel vigorous and virile. Rosella would be getting quite a workout tonight. I thanked my lucky stars that Rosella had been so accommodating after my second wife and my mistress of many years, more an emotional than a sexual companion, had both died unexpectedly within months of each other two years ago. I couldn't be more lucky than to now have Rosella to turn to. But, no, that wasn't fully true. For that brief period, several decades ago, before I had to take over the family responsibilities, I had been happier. I had even been happier than that earlier in my youth when I pursued my interests unfettered.

In recent weeks, I've been coming more and more back to the memories of those too-few happy months that summer that my family had dismissed as a midlife madness—and to my American lover. I wondered now if this was a harbinger of the end of my days. I have just turned seventy, but I'm in as good a condition as considerable money and leisure can buy. My family hasn't been known for its longevity, however. Already the grandchildren I keep around me treat me like a doddering patriarch. It can't be denied that I have become the patriarch of the ancient line of the house of Ghiberti, outliving not only the previous generation but most of my own generation—and that of my children as well. At least I have grandchildren around me, although I must savor Paulo while he's here, before he goes into the priesthood.

It must have been these memories that caused me to pull off the highway and motor into the center of Lucca to break my trip back to Montebella, the family estate in the hills on the coast of Tuscany, above Marina de Massa and the Ligurian Sea. When I'd left Val d'Orcia I could hardly wait to get back to my Tuscan vineyard in the lushest of all seasons, the September grape harvest time, and into Rosella's arms. But the memories—and thinking on that both troubling and arousing letter—had crowded in as I neared Lucca. I found myself homing in on that city's Piazza dell'Anfiteatro—where I had met my American lover all those self-denying years ago.

As I walked into the piazza and toward the Café del Mercato, I wondered if that sidewalk café was still as notorious a pickup spot of a certain kind as it was in my youth. And then, as the café came into view, my heart gave a lurch, and I could feel an awakening in my groin as well.

Could it be? No, that was impossible. He looked just as Daniel had looked that first day, in this same location. But it must have been because of the unexpected letter—just a note, really—now hidden in the secret compartment of the writing desk in my bedroom. It must just be the letter that put the image in my mind to be engraved on the face of any passing beautiful young man of twenty. I looked around the piazza at other men, not seeing Daniel in them. But they were dark-complexioned Italians, like me, not the sunny American blond that was Daniel—and that was this young man sitting at the café.

He was lounging—more than sitting—at the same table, in the same chair, that Daniel, my American lover, had been sitting in when I started into that last, heart-wrenching unspeakable affair. My last carefree hurrah in that year of my father's death—at a younger age than I now was—before my duties to our ancient Tuscan family line had taken over my life and had hardened my heart to my own needs. This young man must be more apparition than reality. He was the same muscular, blond American beauty of my midlife fling—the very same youth. He wasn't a day older than when I'd first seen him shining in the light filtering into the piazza and flashing that open, intoxicating American smile. And yet I was no longer the man at the height of his virility that I had been at forty. Could it be that time stood still for Daniel when it started to rush in the set trenches of family duty for me all those years ago? No, it couldn't be.

I willed myself to just stroll on by the café, to keep tapping my gold-headed cane along the cobblestones and circle back to the car and speed back to Rosella's accommodating arms. But then he smiled at me, that golden all-American boy smile, and my remembrances took hold of my feet and pulled me into the café.

"Excuse me, young man," I said in my well-practiced English. "Is this seat taken?"

"No, it isn't," the young man answered with that glowing smile. "Please, please do join me."

"I'm sorry, but I was arrested by your visage," I said. "You look so much like someone I once knew."

"I'm American," he said, as if that would negate any possibility that we'd previously met.

"Yes, somehow I knew that," I answered. So was he, my young lover of long ago. "Tell me," I continued, "do you, by any chance, have anyone named Daniel in your family? Someone who had visited Italy before?"

"Well, I do have a granduncle with that name," the youth said. "And I do know he traveled in Europe when he was young, but I don't know if he ever was in Italy. I'll have to ask him."

"It seems quite likely he was," I answered, but I didn't explain further when the young man gave me a quizzical look. "And your name, if I might ask?" I didn't want the conversation to end, and I wondered yet again whether this young American had any idea what signals young men—at least local men—customarily were sending by sitting in this spot in this café. I began to be quite conscious of what was going on between my thighs. The waters of the Val d'Orcia had put me into the mood, and the reminisces of my golden summer with Daniel those many years ago had directed that mood down a path I had studiously denied myself for decades.

"I'm Dakota."

"Dakota . . .?" I wanted a surname; I wanted some sort of confirmation of a connection.

"Just Dakota," he said. "I'm traveling through Europe as a vagabond. Just finished college in the States, and it was such a long, hard grind getting to that point that I'm rewarding myself with an autumn of wandering in search of paradise. I think I've found the perfect place for just letting my hair down and letting adventure take me where it will here in Tuscany. Besides, I've reached a stage in my travels when I need a transfusion of funds and my family needs to touch base. This seemed as good a place to meet up with family as any."

"Indeed," I answered. The situation here was still enigmatic. I was receiving what I thought were signals, but did this luscious young man have any notion that signals were even in play here? Did he know what this café was known for?

"I said, and what's your name?" he was saying to me. My thoughts had been elsewhere.

A waiter had come to the table for my order, which had cut through the fog of my ruminating, but I only belatedly noticed the sharp look the young American gave me after the waiter, knowing full well who I was, had practically genuflected to me both in approaching and leaving the table.

"Oh, the long version is that I'm the seventh Conte di Ghiberti of Massa, Tuscany. But you can just call me Luciano, if you like," I answered with a low laugh.

"My, that sounds very impressive and rich—and oddly familiar," he said, his eyes dancing in the sunlight. And did I perceive him move his chair a bit closer to me and lean in more toward me?

"Yes, I'm afraid that is my burden," I responded. And he had no idea what a burden it had been, something that forced me into a life I didn't really want to lead and away from the greatest love of my life—who this blond god before me so strikingly resembled. "I'm afraid my illustrious family goes back in the Tuscan area to a very rich and powerful distant relative and benefactor, Pope Pius V. He somehow inherited Tuscany as a personal duchy and set his favored relatives up in business. The Ghibertis have been entrenched in the hills north of here between the villages of Massa in the vineyard district and Marina de Massa on the Ligurian Sea for the last two centuries. We made our money on silk and banking and have proceeded to spend it on wine and sex—many varieties of sex."

There, I'd sent out a signal of my own, and the young American, Dakota, quite clearly showed that he knew exactly why he'd been sitting in this spot in this particular café. I felt a hand on my knee. It probably was a cool hand, but it felt hot enough to burn its way through the silk fabric of my trousers and brand my thigh for what I'd always known I was.

I hadn't done this for thirty years. But he was so much like Daniel . . . whose letter had started a stirring in me. I didn't even know what these arrangements cost any more. Of course he was an American. He might not know any better what the going rates were in Italy. There wasn't much doubt that he knew we were into negotiations, though. The waiter was watching us from the shadows—he knew too.

"Fascinating," the young man said, turning on that big smile of his again. "I'm just wandering through Italy, taking small jobs where I can to get me to the next village, or otherwise availing myself of the generous hospitality of the . . . men . . . of the region."

"If you are headed north," I said, trying to keep my wits about me and my voice level under the burning hand that was slowly creeping up my thigh, "perhaps you might be interested in availing yourself of my family estate, the Villa Montebella, for a few days."

"That would be super," Dakota was saying, but nearly all of my attention was now centered on his hand, which had reached my basket and was finding that I could be quite hospitable to him indeed.

Both the young man and I froze at the sound of a voice familiar to both of us. "Ah, I thought I might find you here, Dakota. And with Luciano, I see. Quite an attraction the count

118

has to the Wilson men, I see. But let us not interrupt your little cruising expedition, Dakota. Perhaps Luciano will come take a walk with me. You'll have no trouble finding someone else."

Dakota leaned away from me in a slight sulk. I was having more trouble regaining my composure. "So, you two already know each other, Uncle Dan?" the young man said.

"Yes, Luciano and I are friends—very old friends, Dakota. And I'm sure we have much to reminisce about that you wouldn't be interested in. Shall we walk together, old friend, and perhaps find another café where our conversation won't bore young Dakota here?"

I numbly stood and let my older, lover for a summer, Daniel guide me into the piazza and toward the fountain in the center.

* * * *

"Would you have gone with Dakota?" Daniel asked me as we reached the fountain. We stood there, looking at the water cascading down into the pool, me, at least, not focusing on it. He had his arm through mine still and couldn't help but feel me trembling. But perhaps he would take it as the infirmity of old age. He was still a beautiful man, even though he would be fifty now. Trim, still more blond than gray, classic chiseled features that probably never would age. His grip was strong. His grip on me had always been strong.

"I haven't been with another man since that summer, Daniel."

"I'm not surprised. You seemed to be keeping busy and that scandal with the other man's wife—"

I was stunned. He had been following my life. "I did what was expected. When my father died, I became the head of the family. I did what was required. This is Tuscany, Daniel, not New York. We don't live in even the same century here as they do in New York."

"As we do in New York," he said softly.

"Ah." That's where he'd been. He'd kept track of me but I hadn't done so with him.

"But you didn't answer my question," he continued. "Dakota had moved in very close to you before I arrived at the café—and I know what Dakota was looking for in the café. He asked me where to find it and I told him where. I remember the café well, as if it were yesterday. Would you have gone with him?"

"Yes, Probably." I hadn't answered right away. There had been a pause during which I thought not to answer, but I was too weary—and half in shock—to not answer him. And to do so honestly.

"Because he looks so much like I did at that age?"

"Yes. Only for that reason. I received your letter. It was on my mind."

"I had planned on seeing you while I was here," he continued, apparently satisfied—and possibly pleased—at the answer I'd given him, "but not quite as coincidentally as this. I did send that note to put myself back in your mind before I called on you in person."

"Yes, yes, you did. But why now, Daniel? It's been thirty years."

"I suddenly found myself alone."

"A death? A man?"

"Yes. We'd been together nearly those thirty years. The depth of rejection—after what we'd had—and the violence of the men of your family . . . well, I found someone else as soon as I could. And it was a good life. He was reliable. He would fight to keep me."

I felt the sting, but it was justified, so I didn't object to it. "And that was the only reason? You haven't come back to make life difficult for me? I didn't come to you in the hospital—but surely you knew that I couldn't. For your sake, if nothing else. It was bad enough for you as it was."

Daniel didn't answer that, and when he did say something, it was somewhat elliptical. "It wasn't just a fling for me, Luciano. Not like Dakota's come on back there—not just for money, for food, a roof over my head, a quick jack off, and transportation to the next coastal village."

"I know it wasn't. It wasn't anything like that for me either."

"The family did have an arrangement to check up with Dakota and ensure he had the money to go on. He doesn't really have to pimp himself across Europe. He does that because he enjoys it. I'm sure he was offering himself to you because he would enjoy you."

"But it was your idea of meeting him here in Tuscany, wasn't it—not in Berlin or London?" I asked, not wanting to go off on the tangent of my continued attraction to anyone other than him, although I have to admit he was flattering me—and heating me up.

He didn't directly answer that either. "Is there a hotel nearby?" he asked. We both instantly knew why he asked. Neither one of us questioned that we would fuck. I was hard, and he knew it. He had been making good use of his hands as we talked. Such faith he had that I could still fuck—although, my role had always been that of a receiver, and he now knew I could still get hard. He looked robust still.

"We'll go up to the villa. I have my car here."

"The villa? Won't it be crawling with family?"

"I am the patriarch now. The generation before me is gone as is most of my own—and even my children. All I have left on the estate are grandchildren. And no grown men to assert their code. I do as I please, wherever I please." It wasn't buried that deeply in my mind or in what I was saying to him that I was signaling possibilities that went beyond a surreptitious fuck in a hotel room.

* * * *

Daniel gave an appreciative whistle when he saw that I was driving a Lamborghini Murcielago, the fastest production car in existence, and I showed him just how fast it could go as we wound our way up toward Massa in the hills. Among hillsides covered with regular rows of cascading vines, heavy with luscious grapes, aching to be plucked. I was suddenly young again—not just in having a second chance at a similar experience to that family traditions and outraged male uncles had denied me, but, strangely, at having a nearly identical experience to the most arousing and fulfilling experience I'd ever had. I idiotically wondered as I picked up speed on the familiar twisting road up into the hills whether this Daniel could be both as forceful and gentle—and spontaneous—as my Daniel of old had been.

Daniel wasn't helping. He was ensuring his much-belated welcome to Montebella by, first, rubbing my slowly rehardening cock through my silky trousers, and, then, uncovering it and getting it unbelievably hard for a man of my years. If I hadn't been such a skillful driver, and the road had not been so familiar, I'm sure that my trembling at his touch would have put us to tumbling down onto the rock-enclosed terraces cascading down to the sea.

As it was, when I told him we were now on Ghiberti land, he urged me, with a husky voice, to pull off into one of the side access roads, where we kissed deeply and he sucked me off with huge slurping sounds from him and groans and grunts from me. He was as vigorous and insistent and alive as the younger Daniel had been that summer, and I found myself imagining that my lover had returned to me and everything was just as it once was as I watched the silver-laced golden curls on the back of his head billow and bob around between my belly and the Lamborghini's leather-clad steering wheel.

I grabbed the back of his head, running my fingers into the silver-gold curls, raised my pelvis off the leather driver's seat, and cried out to the sun above, as his lips went all the way down to my balls, and I ejaculated into his throat.

I was being foolish, I knew. I had almost to pinch myself to acknowledge that this wasn't Daniel returning to me in the full flower of my youth, but a seasoned, once spurned, lover with many more mixed emotions than that carefree summer we'd spent in each other's arms. I also worried about how much older I must seem to him, although, if I must say so myself, I was still handsome, if mostly gray, and I had managed to keep my body both firm and supple.

My granddaughter, Gabriella, met us at the door of the villa and gave Daniel a look that seemed to pierce right through to the center of him, and then a look of surprise at me, but she kept her tongue. She was a fiery one, with a quick temper and an acid tongue, but I ruled the family with a strong will and a locked cash box now that the generation before me and her own parents were in the grave, and she said nothing. She gave Daniel another look of disdain, and he gave her a look that told me immediately that he would swing more than one way, given the opportunity, and then she led us into one of the dining rooms. She left us then, while we drank a glass of the estate's best wine, and returned shortly, with Rosella in tow, and a quite presentable late meal for two.

As obedient and compliant as always, Rosella just kept her gaze to the floor as she was serving us. She could tell what was transpiring, I was sure. She had certainly heard about my wild youth and that last explosive summer, and, like all good Italian servants and mistresses, she would bend to the flow.

For several moments the look that Daniel had given Gabriella disturbed me. I couldn't let loose of the possibility that Daniel had returned to me as he had with a deeper motivation than just to see me again—even to fuck me again. Our parting had been so abrupt and violent—in what my uncles did to him—that I always feared what effect it had on him and whether if he ever did come back, it would be more from a need, a desire, for vengeance. And the look he gave Gabriella . . . it was like the twisting of a knife in my gut. But why wouldn't he be able to look with lust on a nubile female beauty—I had been married before he was fucking me—and not unhappily so. And I had had my share of mistresses, as he had clearly shown he knew by referring to the Albertini scandal. I wasn't dead to the charms of a woman as well as a man. Why would he be?

The meal done, I left instructions that I was not to be disturbed until morning and guided Daniel up to the master suite, ignoring Gabriella's muttered comment and Rosella's defeated look.

Daniel quickly, masterfully, and completely took control as soon as the heavy oaken door had shut behind us—just as he had always done. His eyes quickly traveled around the large room, drinking in the wealth of the centuries, stopping briefly at a flattering half-finished oil painting of me on an easel beside a fireplace. Portraits of all of the Ghiberti patriarchs down through the ages hung in the hallways of the villa, and I had left the sitting for mine much later than most had. His attention then focused on the huge four-poster bed beside two full-length glassed doors leading to a balcony and looking down through heavily fruited terraces of grape vines to the near-distant Ligurian Sea. It was near dusk in a musk-heavy late September, and the waning rays of the sun were picking out and making luminescent the white and ocher plastered walls and terra-cotta roof tiles of the buildings stepping down from our hilltop prominence to the turquoise Mediterranean waters below.

Daniel tore at my clothes, telling me how nice I was still, saying all of the right things to keep me in need of his power and masterful attention. Not referring to my age at all.

When he had me undressed, he sat me down on the end of the bed, stepped back, and slowly disrobed, showing me a perfectly formed, heavily muscled body every much—in the fantasy of my willingness—as achingly beautiful as the twenty-year-old Daniel had been in my treasured memories. He was horse-hung, with low-hanging, egg-sized balls poking out of a profusion of curly, golden-blond pubic hair. His butt cheeks were bulbous, firm but round as melons. I could hardly wait to get my hands cupped around those butt cheeks and my tongue on his cock.

Nor did he make me wait. He moved right into me. He pushed his cock between my lips and started a quickening rhythm, forcing me initially to gag from the immediacy and unfamiliarity of the act. But I was quick to remember how it had been with Daniel and all those other young Italian studs I'd been with before him during my youth and my ever-so-brief months of freedom from convention, and I cupped his butt cheeks with my hands and very soon had him moaning and sighing his delight.

Remembrances of the pleasure this gave me was quick to return to me as well. When we had established a rhythm, I took my hands from his buttocks and roamed his body. I closed my eyes, and I once again found all of those mounds and crevices that had excited me about my Daniel of old. The same big, taut nipples surrounded with the same coin-sized, rough-textured aureoles. The same surprisingly thick patch of curly blond hair running across his pecs and down his sternum and belly to meet with his thick profusion of pubic hair—the hair on his arms, legs, and chest so blond that it hardly was noticeable to the eye, but was oh so silky to the touch—and enhanced in shimmery effect, rather than diminished it by the mixing in of silvery strands.

He pushed me back onto the bed and was kneeling above my chest now, forcing his cock down into my mouth and throat like a pile driver, trying to get it all inside my mouth. I sputtered and pulled away long enough to beg him to slow down, but just like the twenty-year-old Daniel, he was relentless in his attack.

"Later, later," he said back to me in a throaty voice, just as he had done as a youth. "Big. Make me big now. I want you to feel every inch of my length and width when I show you again what an American stud can do to an Italian count's ass."

I'd already known what an American stud could do to me, I wanted to yell back at him. But I also didn't want him to stop. Daniel had always given it to me rough to start, which had only made his subsequent tender lovemaking all that better.

Daniel was out of my mouth now, and he'd gone down below the edge of the bed and his mouth, and then his tongue, were at my asshole. The rimming, kissing, licking, nibbling and tongue plunging went on for several minutes, and it felt wonderful. Oh, what had I given up for my responsibilities to my family? It had been so long since my body had been this awake, since it had been played so expertly and completely. No woman had done this for me, to me. I almost cried out in grief that I was being given this reminder in the winter of my years of what might have been, what joy I could have had if I had not been so tied to the responsibility and luxury of Tuscany.

And now he was working on stuffing that huge cock of his brutally inside my channel. He had his hands under my buttocks and was rotating my hips back and forth on his huge cock head, pushing himself into me, stretching my entrance. Just like the younger Daniel did. I closed my eyes tightly again and imagined it was the Daniel of old taking me brutally and totally again, just as he had done the day I told him of my impending second marriage and what that meant—my unattached life over. The last time I'd ever seen Daniel. I opened my eyes, and through the haze of my aging pupils, I saw Daniel's beautiful torso again pushing in between my spread thighs. The same strong, rolling muscles. Biceps; pecs; heaving, flat belly. Hard, bobbing nipples and silky, golden torso hair. His ruggedly handsome-featured face was all intensity, painted with the determination to plug my withering hole with his virile, vigorous cock. His silver-blond curls billowed around his head in the waning rays of light reflected up from the Mediterranean waters and through the French windows.

"Daniel, Daniel, Daniel," I sang to myself, and I found myself relaxing. Daniel had returned to me and would be fucking me in that old, wonderful way we had found before that pleased us both.

As the muscles at the center of me relaxed, Daniel's bulbous dick head breached past my ring, and now I was pulling his cock slowly inside myself with ass muscles that never seemed to have forgotten their former master, Daniel. My ass muscles were making love to Daniel's dick as it plowed up me, and he was crying out his pleasure and surprise—surprise that my channel walls were still supple and tight.

"Yeah, yeah. God, that's good. Fuck, you have one sweet ass! Italian ass. Fuck, fuck, FUCK!"

He gathered up my legs with both of his hands and spread me wide, giving him purchase for that last couple of inches of cock. And then he rode me and rode me and rode me. I shot my patrician semen far up his belly long before he had come himself, in fast, furious, relentless strokes deep inside me.

The long-fingered shadows of twilight were creeping into the room through the French doors to the balcony when he'd finished me. He padded off to the toilet, while I just lay there, my chest heaving, trying to catch my breath, and wondering if I was having a heart attack or already was in heaven. I laughed at the thought that I had been excited about the prospect of fucking Rosella tonight after an invigorating visit to the spa. I hadn't even imagined at the time that this would happen to me. I long ago had given up on the idea that I would ever again be doing this, having this done to me.

Daniel padded back into the room and told me what a nice bathroom I had, that it was nearly as big as his whole apartment back in New York City was. I searched his eyes for signs that this fuck just been something from his past life that he'd had to close out on, but, if that's how he felt, he hid it well. Of course, he was probably used to hiding his feelings this way. I'd seen the look he'd given Gabriella, and I suddenly was a little worried having him around. Before I could chew on this thought any further, though, he spoke up.

"Umm. Do you have a place for me to stay tonight, then?"

"Yes," I said, looking directly in his eyes. "Here, in my bed, inside me. You said there would be a more tender encounter later. For reasons I cannot tell you, that's important to me."

"Sounds good to me," he said in an off-hand voice. "Would you like to start in the shower? Yours seems big enough to handle a whole fucking regiment. Or a whole regiment fucking, for that matter." That big, open American smile and laugh again.

We showered together, with him taking the lead on soaping us off, and then getting down on his knees and languidly sucking me off, with his hands strongly holding me at the upper thighs, keeping me from melting into the floor in a tremulous heap at what his mouth was doing to my cock.

He dried us both off. Me first, after which he settled me in the center of my bed and then put on an exhibition of standing in front of me and drying himself off with the thick bath towel. Then he came up on the bed and stretched himself beside me and took my lips in his. His hands roamed my body, and once again his tongue found my asshole, and when he'd gotten me open and wet, he fucked me in a side-split, much more gently this second time, as he had promised and as I had said I wanted. He fucked me from behind and below with both of us resting on our sides, him holding my leg up from my body at first to give his cock close access—just like he had always done before in his tender moments. I drifted off to sleep, a tired, aging man, with that big cock of his gently rocking back and forth inside me. And the last sighed word on my lips before I slept was "Daniel." And it was my beautiful, young, virile Daniel I dreamt about.

I woke before Daniel did. His cock was still inside me and was flaccid. But even when flaccid, it filled me. I was satiated and beginning to worry about what I'd done and how the grandchildren and Rosella would take this erratic behavior on my part and intrusion on Daniel's part. A silly old man, taking a younger stranger into his bed. This was Tuscany, and they were no fools. They knew that the rich and powerful did whatever they wanted here and were eccentric enough to try almost anything. But it had been so long, and I'd never told anyone of the younger generation what I had sacrificed for what the family had established here.

Daniel was coming alive and running his hands around my body now. One of the servants had come in and closed the shutters over the French doors in the night, but strong sunlight was fighting its way between the slats and creating a striped pattern across our naked bodies, mine cuddled inside Daniel's. I watched the palm of Daniel's hand spread across my belly in the alternating shadow and strip of sunlight and felt his dick coming to life inside me.

He nuzzled his lips into the hollow of my neck and intoned, "Again. Once again, hard and deep. Then I want to walk in your vineyard, and then I want to return and plow your soil again. Good, rich Italian soil. You have aged well, Luciano." He kissed me then in the hollow of my neck with a sucking kiss that

132

ended with nibbling of teeth. His spread hand pushed on my belly, pushing my pelvis onto his cock as it lengthened and thickened again. I ached, both physically and psychologically. I truly was too old for repeated deep fuckings, I thought, and I ached for my Daniel. I wanted to be as young and virile as Daniel even now, at fifty, was. To be chasing each other through fecund fields and taking turns in catching and overpowering and fucking each other.

"I don't know, Daniel," I whispered. "I don't know if I have the strength or can muster enough manhood to do it again so soon. Maybe later."

"I have the strength for both of us. I want you again. Now. I felt the doubt in your mind and body last night of whether I enjoyed you, and I want to show you that I did and do—that I can't keep myself away from and out of you."

And he proceeded to show me that I did want him again. I wanted him, Daniel, hardening inside of me, wanting me. Fuck the family and whatever they might think. Fuck feeling my heart beat too fast and having to fight for the next breath. I wanted Daniel and I wanted him now.

"Hard, deep, fast, rough, and close," he whispered into my ear. "I can tell you love it that way no matter what you say." Then he pushed me over on my belly and straddled my thighs with his knees. He ran his hands up my arms and grabbed my wrists and moved my hands up to the iron rods running up the headboard.

"Grab hold of these," he whispered in a husky voice. "You'll need to hang on to something tight. I hope they are strong enough."

Then his dick head was at my tightened hole again, and he was pushing hard into me from behind and above. He had his hands wrapped around to my chest, with his fingers gripping my nipples. Even though my hole had been tightened up by his pressure on my thighs, his cock had made a lasting impression on my ass canal the previous night. So, once his dick head was past the ring, my ass walls were pulling him into me again as before. As soon as he was in up to the root, he started riding me in hard strokes, alternating with rotating hips, that had the mattress bouncing up and down and back and forth wildly and my knuckles white from the effort of grabbing the iron rods at the headboard and holding myself in place under him. He fucked me hard and deep and fast for what seemed to be almost forever, certainly with much more stamina than I'd ever remembered Daniel managing before. After shooting off in three strong ejaculations that bathed my insides completely in his semen, he collapsed on top of me.

"Now that I've explored your sweet ass again, let's shower and explore your vineyard."

"I think you'll have to go on without me," I barely managed to reply. "You've worn me out. I don't think I'll be able to move until noon."

"Noon?" Daniel asked mischievously. "I'm not sure I can hold off on my next visit with you that long."

"I'm sure you can manage, Daniel. The servants will know exactly what you're doing here and will, without challenge, get you something to eat and an escort around the estate. But my granddaughter, Gabriella," I added in a nervous afterthought. "You'd best keep away from that one."

"I hear you," Daniel said, as he rose from the bed and started for the bathroom. And I hoped he had heard me. If he wanted to live in the lap of luxury here at the Villa Montebella for a few days, he'd best concentrate his attention.

"Oh, and my grandson, Paulo," I said. "He's visiting, but you probably won't see much of him. He loves working in the vineyard and spends most of his time there."

"You have a grandson here?" Daniel stopped in his tracks and turned toward me. My cock ached at the sight of his swinging around between his legs.

"Yes, but I don't really want you talking with him at all. He's my younger grandson, headed for the priesthood. My older grandson will inherit all of this, and he's off in Sienna managing our business there. My younger grandson is studying at the seminary now. As I said earlier, we have popes in our lineage and intend to have more popes there."

"Oh, right, a priest; saved for God," Daniel said. And he turned and marched into the bathroom, not letting me see the expression on his face. And it's just as well that I didn't. I drifted

135

off to sleep, and my dreams returned to remembrances of my beloved Daniel. When I woke, my heart pounding, my breath coming in off-beat gasps, reminding me of my age and of my heart condition, Daniel had showered and was gone. And had left me alone in my sunlight-dappled room, an old, tired man, foolishly clamoring to catch some sense of his faded youth.

I heard voices wafting up from the edge of the vineyard below my window. Three men. The sweet innocence of my grandson, Paulo, entertaining a request for a tour of the vineyard. Listening to what was being requested, but in his innocence—or possibly in my jadedness in hearing more than was there—not hearing the double entendres. The other voices, smooth and seductive sliced into me like knives. Daniel . . . and Dakota. Dakota too.

The word "vengeance" screamed through my brain, and I struggled to rise from the bed, but the pounding of the heart in my chest and excruciating pain exploding through my body . . . the gasps . . . I couldn't catch my breath . . . I couldn't . . .

~~

About the Author

Habu is one of the pen names of a former supersonic spy jet pilot, intelligence agent, male model, movie actor, and diplomat. A wild youth in South East Asia was spent enjoying whatever sexual opportunities came his way, and much of his gay male writing is about recalling incidents from those days and inventing ones he'd perhaps have liked to experience. He now leads a very quiet and ordinary happily married family life.

An American, he is a published mainstream novelist and short story writer under another name and in another dimension of his life. He has written or cowritten (with Sabb) approaching 1,000 published short stories and over 100 published erotica e-books, primarily of gay fiction but also memoir, straight fiction and ménage fiction. His hand and creative writing can be seen in stories and books by habu, sr71plt, Dirk Hessian, Shabbu, and Stephen Kessel—among unrevealed others that might surprise readers. The fictionalized GM memoir *Flying High, Diving Deep* is loosely based on his life experiences. He can be found at the adults only gay male site www.BarbarianSpy.com, which he shares with Sabb and Dirk Hessian.

Our authors always like to receive feedback, and appreciate it when readers post reviews at distributors and other sites.

BarbarianSpy

FOR LITERARY HEAT

Not all books listed below may currently be on release.
* indicates the book is available in paperback and e-book.

BOOKS BY DIRK HESSIAN

Xtreme Erotica
The King's Men
Shores of Tripoli
Prophecy of Noto
Pretender's Fate

General Erotica/Romance
Fire Down the Valley*
Constantinople*
The Beautiful Way*
Blue and Gray
Colonel's Treasure
Beginning of Time
Labyrinth

BOOKS BY HABU

Gay Erotica
Memoir Faction
Flying High, Diving Deep*

Xtreme Erotica
Apyko: The Greek Pimp
Visits of the Schlange
Second Coming: Emile La Cour Unleashed
Vortex: Sacrificed by Curiosity*
Dark Angel Sounding *(in e-book & included in Sounding:Ultimate Control Paperback)**
Sounding: Ultimate Control *(Print Only)**
Sounding Five *(in e-book & included in Sounding:Ultimate Control paperback)**

General Erotica
Romance

Trading Partners (Valentine's Day)
Friday Nights with Lenny (Christmas Romance)
Snowy, Snowy Nights (Christmas Romance)
Four Coins
Lower Than the Heart (Valentines Day)
Brambleton
Gotta Keep Trying
Finding Amnad
Platres Conclave
Other Novels/Novellas
Cruising Gigolo (bisexual)
Prepared in Cape Verdi
Gilded Cage
House on Park
Anything for Ambition
Dance of the Ravishers
Hard Knocks U*
My Neighbor's Spa*
Man's Man: Tales of a High Priced Gay Hooker*
Trip Money
Clint Folsom Mysteries Compendium Volume 1*
Death to Blonds - Stolen Judgment (Clint Folsom
Mystery)*
Clint Folsom Mysteries Compendium Volume 2*
The Indian Doctor
Sailorboy
Home to Fire Island
Choke Hold
Gay Erotica Anthologies
Fifty Seventy
Spy Tails 001*
Spy Tails 002*
Doubled*
Doubled Again*
Tails in the Tropics*
Tails in the Med*
Tails in the West*
Rough Riders*

Grab Bag 1*
Grab Bag 2*
Grab Bag 3*
Grab Bag 4*
Grab Bag 5*
Beyond the Beaded Curtain*
Habu's Christmas Balls
The Sporting Life*
Fetish Galore!*
Literary Gay Erotica
Cairo Surrender*
The Handyman*
Homeward Bound
Journey to Mirage*
Menage Erotica
Cruising Gigolo
13 Ways for Halloween
Luther*
The Indian Prince
Literary GLBT Fiction
Summer of Denial
BOOKS BY SHABBU
Velvet Interrogation
Finding Jason
Dirty Pool
Operation Black Jade
Cigars!*
Angel in the Barn
Gayly Complicated*
Despoiling David
The Tree of Idleness*
I Met a Man
Rough Road to Happiness
BOOKS BY SABB
Hiring in Hollywood
The Legend of Holleystone Grange
Surprise Encounters
She is He

Wrong Man
Loyal to his King
Barbarian Tales - Book One - Traveler's Tales*
Barbarian Tales - Book Two - Journeys Begin*
Barbarian Tales - Book Three - The Inheritance*
Barbarian Tales - Book Four - Road to Persepolis*

www.ingramcontent.com/pod-product-compliance
Lightning Source LLC
Chambersburg PA
CBHW051842170626
46807CB00003B/1314